THE APPLE-TREE TABLE, AND OTHER SKETCHES

By Herman Melville

NATAL PUBLISHING LLC
ARS LONGA, VITA BREVIS

Copyright© 2024 Natal Publishing

All rights reserved

OR ORIGINAL SPIRITUAL MANIFESTATIONS

When I first saw the table, dingy and dusty, in the furthest corner of the old hopper-shaped garret, and set out with broken, be-crusted old purple vials and flasks, and a ghostly, dismantled old quarto, it seemed just such a necromantic little old table as might have belonged to Friar Bacon. Two plain features it had, significant of conjurations and charms—the circle and tripod; the slab being round, supported by a twisted little pillar, which, about a foot from the bottom, sprawled out into three crooked legs, terminating in three cloven feet. A very satanic-looking little old table, indeed.

In order to convey a better idea of it, some account may as well be given of the place it came from. A very old garret of a very old house in an old-fashioned quarter of one of the oldest towns in America. This garret had been closed for years. It was thought to be haunted; a rumor, I confess, which, however absurd (in my opinion), I did not, at the time of purchasing, very vehemently contradict; since, not improbably, it tended to place the property the more conveniently within my means.

It was, therefore, from no dread of the reputed goblins aloft, that, for five years after first taking up my residence in the house, I never entered the garret. There was no special inducement. The roof was well slated, and thoroughly tight. The company that insured the house, waived all visitation of the garret; why, then, should the owner be over-anxious about it?—particularly, as he had no use for it, the house having ample room below. Then the key of the stair-door leading to it was lost. The lock was a huge old-fashioned one. To open it, a smith would have to be called; an unnecessary trouble, I thought. Besides, though I had taken some care to keep my two daughters in ignorance of the rumor above-mentioned, still, they had, by some means, got an inkling of it, and were well enough pleased to see the entrance to the haunted ground closed. It might have remained so for a still longer time, had it not been for my accidentally discovering, in a corner of our glen-like, old, terraced garden, a large and curious key, very old and rusty, which I at once concluded must belong to the garret-door—a supposition which, upon trial, proved correct. Now, the possession of a key to anything, at once provokes a desire to unlock and explore; and this, too, from a mere instinct of gratification, irrespective of any particular benefit to accrue.

Behold me, then, turning the rusty old key, and going up, alone, into the haunted garret. It embraced the entire area of the mansion. Its ceiling was formed by the roof, showing the rafters and boards on which the slates were laid. The roof shedding the water four ways from a high point in the centre, the space beneath was much like that of a general's marquee—only midway broken by a labyrinth of timbers, for braces, from which waved innumerable cobwebs, that, of a summer's noon, shone like Bagdad tissues and gauzes. On every hand, some strange insect was seen, flying, or running, or creeping, on rafter and floor.

Under the apex of the roof was a rude, narrow, decrepit step-ladder, something like a Gothic pulpit-stairway, leading to a pulpit-like platform, from which a still narrower ladder—a sort of Jacob's ladder—led somewhat higher to the lofty scuttle. The slide of this scuttle was about two feet square, all in one piece, furnishing a massive frame for a single small pane of glass, inserted into it like a bull's-eye. The light of the garret came from this sole source, filtrated through a dense curtain of cobwebs. Indeed, the whole stairs, and platform, and ladder, were festooned, and carpeted, and canopied with cobwebs; which, in funereal accumulations, hung, too, from the groined, murky ceiling, like the Carolina moss in the cypress forest. In these cobwebs, swung, as in aerial catacombs, myriads of all tribes of mummied insects.

Climbing the stairs to the platform, and pausing there, to recover my breath, a curious scene was presented. The sun was about half-way up. Piercing the little sky-light, it slopingly bored a rainbowed tunnel clear across the darkness of the garret. Here, millions of butterfly moles were swarming. Against the sky-light itself, with a cymbal-like buzzing, thousands of insects clustered in a golden mob.

Wishing to shed a clearer light through the place, I sought to withdraw the scuttle-slide. But no sign of latch or hasp was visible. Only after long peering, did I discover a little padlock, imbedded, like an oyster at the bottom of the sea, amid matted masses of weedy webs, chrysalides, and insectivorous eggs. Brushing these away, I found it locked. With a crooked nail, I tried to pick the lock, when scores of small ants and flies, half-torpid, crawled forth from the keyhole, and, feeling the warmth of the sun in the pane, began frisking around me. Others appeared. Presently, I was overrun by them. As if incensed at this invasion of their retreat, countless bands darted up from below, beating about my head, like hornets. At last, with a sudden jerk, I burst open the scuttle. And ah! what a change. As from the gloom of the grave and the companionship of worms, men shall at last rapturously rise into the living greenness and glory-immortal, so, from my cobwebbed old garret, I thrust forth my head into the balmy air, and found myself hailed by the verdant tops of great trees, growing in the little garden below—trees, whose leaves soared high above my topmost slate.

Refreshed by this outlook, I turned inward to behold the garret, now unwontedly lit up. Such humped masses of obsolete furniture. An old escritoire, from whose pigeon-holes sprang mice, and from whose secret drawers came subterranean squeakings, as from chipmunks' holes in the woods; and broken-down old chairs, with strange carvings, which seemed fit to seat a conclave of conjurors. And a rusty, iron-bound chest, lidless, and packed full of mildewed old documents; one of which, with a faded red ink-blot at the end, looked as if it might have been the original bond that Doctor Faust gave to Mephistopheles. And, finally, in the least lighted corner of all, where was a profuse litter of indescribable old rubbish—among which was a broken telescope, and a celestial globe staved in—stood the little old table, one hoofed foot, like that of the Evil One, dimly revealed through the cobwebs. What a thick dust, half paste, had settled upon the old vials and flasks; how their once liquid contents had caked, and how strangely looked the mouldy old book in the middle—Cotton Mather's *Magnalia*.

Table and book I removed below, and had the dislocations of the one and the tatters of the other repaired. I resolved to surround this sad little hermit of a table, so long banished from genial neighborhood, with all the kindly influences of warm urns, warm fires, and warm hearts, little dreaming what all this warm nursing would hatch.

I was pleased by the discovery that the table was not of the ordinary mahogany, but of apple-tree-wood, which age had darkened nearly to walnut. It struck me as being an appropriate piece of furniture for our cedar-parlor—so called, from its being, after the old fashion, wainscoted with that wood. The table's round slab, or orb, was so contrived as to be readily changed from a horizontal to a perpendicular position; so that, when not in use, it could be snugly placed in a corner. For myself, wife, and two daughters, I thought it would make a nice little breakfast and tea-table. It was just the thing for a whist-table, too. And I also pleased myself with the idea that it would make a famous reading-table.

In these fancies, my wife, for one, took little interest. She disrelished the idea of so unfashionable and indigent-looking a stranger as the table intruding into the polished society of more prosperous furniture. But when, after seeking its fortune at the cabinet-maker's, the table came home, varnished over, bright as a guinea, no one exceeded my wife in a gracious reception of it. It was advanced to an honorable position in the cedar-parlor.

But, as for my daughter Julia, she never got over her strange emotions upon first accidentally encountering the table. Unfortunately, it was just as I was in the act of bringing it down from the garret. Holding it by the slab, I was carrying it before me, one cobwebbed hoof thrust out, which weird object at a turn of the stairs, suddenly touched my girl, as she was ascending; whereupon, turning, and seeing no living creature—for I was quite hidden behind my shield—seeing nothing indeed, but the apparition of the Evil One's foot, as it seemed, she cried out, and there is no knowing what might have followed, had I not immediately spoken.

From the impression thus produced, my poor girl, of a very nervous temperament, was long recovering. Superstitiously grieved at my violating the forbidden solitude above, she associated in her mind the cloven-footed table with the reputed goblins there. She besought me to give up the idea of domesticating the table. Nor did her sister fail to add her entreaties. Between my girls there was a constitutional sympathy. But my matter-of-fact wife had now declared in the table's favor. She was not wanting in firmness and energy. To her, the prejudices of Julia and Anna were simply ridiculous. It was her maternal duty, she thought, to drive such weakness away. By degrees, the girls, at breakfast and tea, were induced to sit down with us at the table. Continual proximity was not without effect. By and by, they would sit pretty tranquilly, though Julia, as much as possible, avoided glancing at the hoofed feet, and, when at this I smiled, she would look at me seriously—as much as to say, Ah, papa, you, too, may yet do the same. She prophesied that, in connection with the table, something strange would yet happen. But I would only smile the more, while my wife indignantly chided.

Meantime, I took particular satisfaction in my table, as a night reading-table. At a ladies' fair, I bought me a beautifully worked reading-cushion, and, with elbow leaning thereon, and hand shading my eyes from the light, spent many a long hour—nobody by, but the queer old book I had brought down from the garret.

All went well, till the incident now about to be given—an incident, be it remembered, which, like every other in this narration, happened long before the time of the "Fox Girls."

It was late on a Saturday night in December. In the little old cedar-parlor, before the little old apple-tree table, I was sitting up, as usual, alone. I had made more than one effort to get up and go to bed; but I could not. I was, in fact, under a sort of fascination. Somehow, too, certain reasonable opinions of mine, seemed not so reasonable as before. I felt nervous. The truth was, that though, in my previous night-readings, Cotton Mather had but amused me, upon this particular night he terrified me. A thousand times I had laughed at such stories. Old wives' fables, I thought, however entertaining. But now, how different. They began to put on the aspect of reality. Now, for the first time it struck me that this was no romantic Mrs. Radcliffe, who had written the *Magnalia*; but a practical, hard-working, earnest, upright man, a learned doctor, too, as well as a good Christian and orthodox clergyman. What possible motive could such a man have to deceive? His style had all the plainness and unpoetic boldness of truth. In the most straightforward way, he laid before me detailed accounts of New England witchcraft, each important item corroborated by respectable townsfolk, and, of not a few of the most surprising, he himself had been eye-witness. Cotton Mather testified himself whereof he had seen. But, is it possible? I asked myself. Then I remembered that Dr. Johnson, the matter-of-fact compiler of a dictionary, had been a believer in ghosts, besides many other sound, worthy men. Yielding to the fascination, I read deeper and deeper into the night. At last, I found myself starting at the least chance sound, and yet wishing that it were not so very still.

A tumbler of warm punch stood by my side, with which beverage, in a moderate way, I was accustomed to treat myself every Saturday night; a habit, however, against which my good wife had long remonstrated; predicting that, unless I gave it up, I would yet die a miserable sot. Indeed, I may here mention that, on the Sunday mornings following my Saturday nights, I had to be exceedingly cautious how I gave way to the slightest impatience at any accidental annoyance; because such impatience was sure to be quoted against me as evidence of the melancholy consequences of over-night indulgence. As for my wife, she, never sipping punch, could yield to any little passing peevishness as much as she pleased.

But, upon the night in question, I found myself wishing that, instead of my usual mild mixture, I had concocted some potent draught. I felt the need of stimulus. I wanted something to hearten me against Cotton Mather—doleful, ghostly, ghastly Cotton Mather. I grew more and more nervous. Nothing but fascination kept me from fleeing the room. The candles burnt low, with long snuffs, and huge winding-sheets. But I durst not raise the snuffers to them. It would make too much noise. And yet, previously, I had been wishing for noise. I read on and on. My hair began to have a sensation. My eyes felt strained; they pained me. I was conscious of it. I knew I was injuring them. I knew I should rue this abuse of them next day; but I read on and on. I could not help it. The skinny hand was on me.

All at once—Hark!

My hair felt like growing grass.

A faint sort of inward rapping or rasping—a strange, inexplicable sound, mixed with a slight kind of wood-pecking or ticking.

Tick! Tick!

Yes, it was a faint sort of ticking.

I looked up at my great Strasbourg clock in one corner. It was not that. The clock had stopped.

Tick! Tick!

Was it my watch?

According to her usual practice at night, my wife had, upon retiring, carried my watch off to our chamber to hang it up on its nail.

I listened with all my ears.

Tick! Tick!

Was it a death-tick in the wainscot?

With a tremulous step I went all round the room, holding my ear to the wainscot.

No; it came not from the wainscot.

Tick! Tick!

I shook myself. I was ashamed of my fright.

Tick! Tick!

It grew in precision and audibleness. I retreated from the wainscot. It seemed advancing to meet me.

I looked round and round, but saw nothing, only one cloven foot of the little apple-tree table.

Bless me, said I to myself, with a sudden revulsion, it must be very late; ain't that my wife calling me? Yes, yes; I must to bed. I suppose all is locked up. No need to go the rounds.

The fascination had departed, though the fear had increased. With trembling hands, putting Cotton Mather out of sight, I soon found myself, candlestick in hand, in my chamber, with a peculiar rearward feeling, such as some truant dog may feel. In my eagerness to get well into the chamber, I stumbled against a chair.

"Do try and make less noise, my dear," said my wife from the bed.

"You have been taking too much of that punch, I fear. That sad habit grows on you. Ah, that I should ever see you thus staggering at night into your chamber."

"Wife," hoarsely whispered I, "there is—is something tick-ticking in the cedar-parlor."

"Poor old man—quite out of his mind—I knew it would be so. Come to bed; come and sleep it off."

"Wife, wife!"

"Do, do come to bed. I forgive you. I won't remind you of it to-morrow. But you must give up the punch-drinking, my dear. It quite gets the better of you."

"Don't exasperate me," I cried now, truly beside myself; "I will quit the house!"

"No, no! not in that state. Come to bed, my dear. I won't say another word."

The next morning, upon waking, my wife said nothing about the past night's affair, and, feeling no little embarrassment myself, especially at having been thrown into such a panic, I also was silent. Consequently, my wife must still have ascribed my singular conduct to a mind disordered, not by ghosts, but by punch. For my own part, as I lay in bed watching the sun in the panes, I began to think that much midnight reading of Cotton Mather was not good for man; that it had a morbid influence upon the nerves, and gave rise to hallucinations. I resolved to put Cotton Mather permanently aside. That done, I had no fear of any return of the ticking. Indeed, I began to think that what seemed the ticking in the room, was nothing but a sort of buzzing in my ear.

As is her wont, my wife having preceded me in rising, I made a deliberate and agreeable toilet. Aware that most disorders of the mind have their origin in the state of the body, I made vigorous use of the flesh-brush, and bathed my head with New England rum, a specific once recommended to me as good for buzzing in the ear. Wrapped in my dressing gown, with cravat nicely adjusted, and fingernails neatly trimmed, I complacently descended to the little cedar-parlor to breakfast.

What was my amazement to find my wife on her knees, rummaging about the carpet nigh the little apple-tree table, on which the morning meal was laid, while my daughters, Julia and Anna, were running about the apartment distracted.

"Oh, papa, papa!" cried Julia, hurrying up to me, "I knew it would be so. The table, the table!"

"Spirits! spirits!" cried Anna, standing far away from it, with pointed finger.

"Silence!" cried my wife. "How can I hear it, if you make such a noise? Be still. Come here, husband; was this the ticking you spoke of? Why don't you move? Was this it? Here, kneel down and listen to it. Tick, tick, tick!—don't you hear it now?"

"I do, I do," cried I, while my daughters besought us both to come away from the spot.

Tick, tick, tick!

Right from under the snowy cloth, and the cheerful urn, and the smoking milk-toast, the unaccountable ticking was heard.

"Ain't there a fire in the next room, Julia," said I, "let us breakfast there, my dear," turning to my wife—"let us go—leave the table—tell Biddy to remove the things."

And so saying I was moving towards the door in high self-possession, when my wife interrupted me.

"Before I quit this room, I will see into this ticking," she said with energy.

"It is something that can be found out, depend upon it. I don't believe in spirits, especially at breakfast-time. Biddy! Biddy! Here, carry these things back to the kitchen," handing the urn. Then, sweeping off the cloth, the little table lay bare to the eye.

"It's the table, the table!" cried Julia.

"Nonsense," said my wife, "Who ever heard of a ticking table? It's on the floor. Biddy! Julia! Anna! move everything out of the room—table and all. Where are the tack-hammers?"

"Heavens, mamma—you are not going to take up the carpet?" screamed Julia.

"Here's the hammers, marm," said Biddy, advancing tremblingly.

"Hand them to me, then," cried my wife; for poor Biddy was, at long gun-distance, holding them out as if her mistress had the plague.

"Now, husband, do you take up that side of the carpet, and I will this." Down on her knees she then dropped, while I followed suit.

The carpet being removed, and the ear applied to the naked floor, not the slightest ticking could be heard.

"The table—after all, it is the table," cried my wife. "Biddy, bring it back."

"Oh no, marm, not I, please, marm," sobbed Biddy.

"Foolish creature!—Husband, do you bring it."

"My dear," said I, "we have plenty of other tables; why be so particular?"

"Where is that table?" cried my wife, contemptuously, regardless of my gentle remonstrance.

"In the wood-house, marm. I put it away as far as ever I could, marm," sobbed Biddy.

"Shall I go to the wood-house for it, or will you?" said my wife, addressing me in a frightful, businesslike manner.

Immediately I darted out of the door, and found the little apple-tree table, upside down, in one of my chip-bins. I hurriedly returned with it, and once more my wife examined it attentively. Tick, tick, tick! Yes, it was the table.

"Please, marm," said Biddy, now entering the room, with hat and shawl—"please, marm, will you pay me my wages?"

"Take your hat and shawl off directly," said my wife; "set this table again."

"Set it," roared I, in a passion, "set it, or I'll go for the police."

"Heavens! heavens!" cried my daughters, in one breath. "What will become of us!—Spirits! spirits!"

"Will you set the table?" cried I, advancing upon Biddy.

"I will, I will—yes, marm—yes, master—I will, I will. Spirits!—Holy Vargin!"

"Now, husband," said my wife, "I am convinced that, whatever it is that causes this ticking, neither the ticking nor the table can hurt us; for we are all good Christians, I hope. I am determined to find out the cause of it, too, which time and patience will bring to light. I shall breakfast on no other table but this, so long as we live in this house. So, sit down, now that all things are ready again, and let us quietly breakfast. My dears," turning to Julia and Anna, "go to your room, and return composed. Let me have no more of this childishness."

Upon occasion my wife was mistress in her house.

During the meal, in vain was conversation started again and again; in vain my wife said something brisk to infuse into others an animation akin to her own. Julia and Anna, with heads bowed over their tea-cups, were still listening for the tick. I confess, too, that their example was catching. But, for the time, nothing was heard. Either the ticking had died quite away, or else, slight as it was, the increasing uproar of the street, with the general hum of day so contrasted with the repose of night and early morning, smothered the sound. At the lurking inquietude of her companions, my wife was indignant; the more so, as she seemed to glory in her own exemption from panic. When breakfast was cleared away she took my watch, and, placing it on the table, addressed the supposed spirits in it, with a jocosely defiant air:

"There, tick away, let us see who can tick loudest!"

All that day, while abroad, I thought of the mysterious table. Could Cotton Mather speak true? Were there spirits? And would spirits haunt a tea-table? Would the Evil One dare show his cloven foot in the bosom of an innocent family? I shuddered when I thought that I myself, against the solemn warnings of my daughters, had wilfully introduced the cloven foot there. Yea, three cloven feet. But, towards noon, this sort of feeling began to wear off. The continual rubbing against so many practical people in the street, brushed such chimeras away from me. I remembered that I had not acquitted myself very intrepidly either on the previous night or in the morning. I resolved to regain the good opinion of my wife.

To evince my hardihood the more signally, when tea was dismissed, and the three rubbers of whist had been played, and no ticking had been heard—which the more encouraged me—I took my pipe, and, saying that bed-time had arrived for the rest, drew my chair towards the fire, and, removing my slippers, placed my feet on the fender, looking as calm and composed as old Democritus in the tombs of Abdera, when one midnight the mischievous little boys of the town tried to frighten that sturdy philosopher with spurious ghosts.

And I thought to myself, that the worthy old gentleman had set a good example to all times in his conduct on that occasion. For, when at the dead hour, intent on his studies, he heard the strange sounds, he did not so much as move his eyes from his page, only simply said: "Boys, little boys, go home. This is no place for you. You will catch cold here." The philosophy of which words lies here: that they imply the foregone conclusion, that any possible investigation of any possible spiritual phenomena was absurd; that upon the first face of such things, the mind of a sane man instinctively affirmed them a humbug, unworthy the least attention; more especially if such phenomena appear in tombs, since tombs are peculiarly the place of silence, lifelessness, and solitude; for which cause, by the way, the old man, as upon the occasion in question, made the tombs of Abdera his place of study.

Presently I was alone, and all was hushed. I laid down my pipe, not feeling exactly tranquil enough now thoroughly to enjoy it. Taking up one of the newspapers, I began, in a nervous, hurried sort of way, to read by the light of a candle placed on a small stand drawn close to the fire. As for the apple-tree table, having lately concluded that it was rather too low for a reading-table, I thought best not to use it as such that night. But it stood not very distant in the middle of the room.

Try as I would, I could not succeed much at reading. Somehow I seemed all ear and no eye; a condition of intense auricular suspense. But ere long it was broken.

Tick! tick! tick!

Though it was not the first time I had heard that sound; nay, though I had made it my particular business on this occasion to wait for that sound, nevertheless, when it came, it seemed unexpected, as if a cannon had boomed through the window.

Tick! tick! tick!

I sat stock still for a time, thoroughly to master, if possible, my first discomposure. Then rising, I looked pretty steadily at the table; went up to it pretty steadily; took hold of it pretty steadily; but let it go pretty quickly; then paced up and down, stopping every moment or two, with ear pricked to listen. Meantime, within me, the contest between panic and philosophy remained not wholly decided.

Tick! tick! tick!

With appalling distinctness the ticking now rose on the night.

My pulse fluttered—my heart beat. I hardly know what might not have followed, had not Democritus just then come to the rescue. For shame, said I to myself, what is the use of so fine an example of philosophy, if it cannot be followed? Straightway I resolved to imitate it, even to the old sage's occupation and attitude.

Resuming my chair and paper, with back presented to the table, I remained thus for a time, as if buried in study, when, the ticking still continuing, I drawled out, in as indifferent and dryly jocose a way as I could; "Come, come, Tick, my boy, fun enough for to-night."

Tick! tick! tick!

There seemed a sort of jeering defiance in the ticking now. It seemed to exult over the poor affected part I was playing. But much as the taunt stung me, it only stung me into persistence. I resolved not to abate one whit in my mode of address.

"Come, come, you make more and more noise, Tick, my boy; too much of a joke—time to have done."

No sooner said than the ticking ceased. Never was responsive obedience more exact. For the life of me, I could not help turning round upon the table, as one would upon some reasonable being, when—could I believe my senses? I saw something moving, or wriggling, or squirming upon the slab of the table. It shone like a glow-worm. Unconsciously, I grasped the poker that stood at hand. But bethinking me how absurd to attack a glow-worm with a poker, I put it down. How long I sat spellbound and staring there, with my body presented one way and my face another, I cannot say; but at length I rose, and, buttoning my coat up and down, made a sudden intrepid forced march full upon the table. And there, near the centre of the slab, as I live, I saw an irregular little hole, or, rather, short nibbled sort of crack, from which (like a butterfly escaping its chrysalis) the sparkling object, whatever it might be, was struggling. Its motion was the motion of life. I stood becharmed. Are there, indeed, spirits, thought I; and is this one? No; I must be dreaming. I turned my glance off to the red fire on the hearth, then back to the pale lustre on the table. What I saw was no optical illusion, but a real marvel. The tremor was increasing, when, once again, Democritus befriended me. Supernatural coruscation as it appeared, I strove to look at the strange object in a purely scientific way. Thus viewed, it appeared some new sort of small shining beetle or bug, and, I thought, not without something of a hum to it, too.

I still watched it, and with still increasing self-possession. Sparkling and wriggling, it still continued its throes. In another moment it was just on the point of escaping its prison. A thought struck me. Running for a tumbler, I clapped it over the insect just in time to secure it.

After watching it a while longer under the tumbler, I left all as it was, and, tolerably composed, retired.

Now, for the soul of me, I could not, at that time, comprehend the phenomenon. A live bug come out of a dead table? A fire-fly bug come out of a piece of ancient lumber, for one knows not how many years stored away in an old garret? Was ever such a thing heard of, or even dreamed of? How got the bug there? Never mind. I bethought me of Democritus, and resolved to keep cool. At all events, the mystery of the ticking was explained. It was simply the sound of the gnawing and filing, and tapping of the bug, in eating its way out. It was satisfactory to think, that there was an end forever to the ticking. I resolved not to let the occasion pass without reaping some credit from it.

"Wife," said I, next morning, "you will not be troubled with any more ticking in our table. I have put a stop to all that."

"Indeed, husband," said she, with some incredulity.

The Apple-Tree Table, and Other Sketches

"Yes, wife," returned I, perhaps a little vaingloriously, "I have put a quietus upon that ticking. Depend upon it, the ticking will trouble you no more."

In vain she besought me to explain myself. I would not gratify her; being willing to balance any previous trepidation I might have betrayed, by leaving room now for the imputation of some heroic feat whereby I had silenced the ticking. It was a sort of innocent deceit by implication, quite harmless, and, I thought, of utility.

But when I went to breakfast, I saw my wife kneeling at the table again, and my girls looking ten times more frightened than ever.

"Why did you tell me that boastful tale," said my wife, indignantly. "You might have known how easily it would be found out. See this crack, too; and here is the ticking again, plainer than ever."

"Impossible," I explained; but upon applying my ear, sure enough, tick! tick! tick! The ticking was there.

Recovering myself the best way I might, I demanded the bug.

"Bug?" screamed Julia, "Good heavens, papa!"

"I hope sir, you have been bringing no bugs into this house," said my wife, severely.

"The bug, the bug!" I cried; "the bug under the tumbler."

"Bugs in tumblers!" cried the girls; "not *our* tumblers, papa? You have not been putting bugs into our tumblers? Oh, what does—what *does* it all mean?"

"Do you see this hole, this crack here?" said I, putting my finger on the spot.

"That I do," said my wife, with high displeasure. "And how did it come there? What have you been doing to the table?"

"Do you see this crack?" repeated I, intensely.

"Yes, yes," said Julia; "that was what frightened me so; it looks so like witch-work."

"Spirits! spirits!" cried Anna.

"Silence!" said my wife. "Go on, sir, and tell us what you know of the crack."

"Wife and daughters," said I, solemnly, "out of that crack, or hole, while I was sitting all alone here last night, a wonderful—"

Here, involuntarily, I paused, fascinated by the expectant attitudes and bursting eyes of Julia and Anna.

"What, what?" cried Julia.

"A bug, Julia."

13

"Bug?" cried my wife. "A bug come out of this table? And what did you do with it?"

"Clapped it under a tumbler."

"Biddy! Biddy!" cried my wife, going to the door. "Did you see a tumbler here on this table when you swept the room?"

"Sure I did, marm, and 'bomnable bug under it."

"And what did you do with it?" demanded I.

"Put the bug in the fire, sir, and rinsed out the tumbler ever so many times, marm."

"Where is that tumbler?" cried Anna. "I hope you scratched it—marked it some way. I'll never drink out of that tumbler; never put it before me, Biddy. A bug—a bug! Oh, Julia! Oh, mamma! I feel it crawling all over me, even now. Haunted table!"

"Spirits! spirits!" cried Julia.

"My daughters," said their mother, with authority in her eyes, "go to your chamber till you can behave more like reasonable creatures. Is it a bug—a bug that can frighten you out of what little wits you ever had? Leave the room. I am astonished, I am pained by such childish conduct."

"Now tell me," said she, addressing me, as soon as they had withdrawn, "now tell me truly, did a bug really come out of this crack in the table?"

"Wife, it is even so."

"Did you see it come out?"

"I did."

She looked earnestly at the crack, leaning over it.

"Are you sure?" said she, looking up, but still bent over.

"Sure, sure."

She was silent. I began to think that the mystery of the thing began to tell even upon her. Yes, thought I, I shall presently see my wife shaking and shuddering, and, who knows, calling in some old dominie to exorcise the table, and drive out the spirits.

"I'll tell you what we'll do," said she suddenly, and not without excitement.

"What, wife?" said I, all eagerness, expecting some mystical proposition; "what, wife?"

"We will rub this table all over with that celebrated 'roach powder' I've heard of."

"Good gracious! Then you don't think it's spirits?"

"Spirits?"

The emphasis of scornful incredulity was worthy of Democritus himself.

"But this ticking—this ticking?" said I.

"I'll whip that out of it."

"Come, come, wife," said I, "you are going too far the other way, now. Neither roach powder nor whipping will cure this table. It's a queer table, wife; there's no blinking it."

"I'll have it rubbed, though," she replied, "well rubbed;" and calling Biddy, she bade her get wax and brush, and give the table a vigorous manipulation. That done, the cloth was again laid, and we sat down to our morning meal; but my daughters did not make their appearance. Julia and Anna took no breakfast that day.

When the cloth was removed, in a businesslike way, my wife went to work with a dark colored cement, and hermetically closed the little hole in the table.

My daughters looking pale, I insisted upon taking them out for a walk that morning, when the following conversation ensued:

"My worst presentiments about that table are being verified, papa," said Julia; "not for nothing was that intimation of the cloven foot on my shoulder."

"Nonsense," said I. "Let us go into Mrs. Brown's, and have an ice-cream."

The spirit of Democritus was stronger on me now. By a curious coincidence, it strengthened with the strength of the sunlight.

"But is it not miraculous," said Anna, "how a bug should come out of a table?"

"Not at all, my daughter. It is a very common thing for bugs to come out of wood. You yourself must have seen them coming out of the ends of the billets on the hearth."

"Ah, but that wood is almost fresh from the woodland. But the table is at least a hundred years old."

"What of that?" said I, gayly. "Have not live toads been found in the hearts of dead rocks, as old as creation?"

"Say what you will, papa, I feel it is spirits," said Julia. "Do, do now, my dear papa, have that haunted table removed from the house."

"Nonsense," said I.

By another curious coincidence, the more they felt frightened, the more I felt brave.

Evening came.

"This ticking," said my wife; "do you think that another bug will come of this continued ticking?"

Curiously enough, that had not occurred to me before. I had not thought of there being twins of bugs. But now, who knew; there might be even triplets.

I resolved to take precautions, and, if there was to be a second bug, infallibly secure it. During the evening, the ticking was again heard. About ten o'clock I clapped a tumbler over the spot, as near as I could judge of it by my ear. Then we all retired, and locking the door of the cedar-parlor, I put the key in my pocket.

In the morning, nothing was to be seen, but the ticking was heard. The trepidation of my daughters returned. They wanted to call in the neighbors. But to this my wife was vigorously opposed. We should be the laughing-stock of the whole town. So it was agreed that nothing should be disclosed. Biddy received strict charges; and, to make sure, was not allowed that week to go to confession, lest she should tell the priest.

I stayed home all that day; every hour or two bending over the table, both eye and ear. Towards night, I thought the ticking grew more distinct, and seemed divided from my ear by a thinner and thinner partition of the wood. I thought, too, that I perceived a faint heaving up, or bulging of the wood, in the place where I had placed the tumbler. To put an end to the suspense, my wife proposed taking a knife and cutting into the wood there; but I had a less impatient plan; namely, that she and I should sit up with the table that night, as, from present symptoms, the bug would probably make its appearance before morning. For myself, I was curious to see the first advent of the thing—the first dazzle of the chick as it chipped the shell.

The idea struck my wife not unfavorably. She insisted that both Julia and Anna should be of the party, in order that the evidence of their senses should disabuse their minds of all nursery nonsense. For that spirits should tick, and that spirits should take unto themselves the form of bugs, was, to my wife, the most foolish of all foolish imaginations. True, she could not account for the thing; but she had all confidence that it could be, and would yet be, somehow explained, and that to her entire satisfaction. Without knowing it herself, my wife was a female Democritus. For my part, my present feelings were of a mixed sort. In a strange and not unpleasing way, I gently oscillated between Democritus and Cotton Mather. But to my wife and daughters I assumed to be pure Democritus—a jeerer at all tea-table spirits whatever.

So, laying in a good supply of candles and crackers, all four of us sat up with the table, and at the same time sat round it. For a while my wife and I carried on an animated conversation. But my daughters were silent. Then my wife and I would have had a rubber of whist, but my daughters could not be prevailed upon to join. So we played whist with two dummies literally; my wife won the rubber and, fatigued with victory, put away the cards.

Half past eleven o'clock. No sign of the bug. The candles began to burn dim. My wife was just in the act of snuffing them, when a sudden, violent, hollow, resounding, rumbling, thumping was heard.

Julia and Anna sprang to their feet.

"All well!" cried a voice from the street. It was the watchman, first ringing down his club on the pavement, and then following it up with this highly satisfactory verbal announcement.

"All well! Do you hear that, my girls?" said I, gayly.

Indeed it was astonishing how brave as Bruce I felt in company with three women, and two of them half frightened out of their wits.

I rose for my pipe, and took a philosophic smoke.

Democritus forever, thought I.

In profound silence, I sat smoking, when lo!—pop! pop! pop!—right under the table, a terrible popping.

This time we all four sprang up, and my pipe was broken.

"Good heavens! what's that?"

"Spirits! spirits!" cried Julia.

"Oh, oh, oh!" cried Anna.

"Shame!" said my wife, "it's that new bottled cider, in the cellar, going off. I told Biddy to wire the bottles to-day."

I shall here transcribe from memoranda, kept during part of the night.

"*One o'clock. No sign of the bug. Ticking continues. Wife getting sleepy.*

"*Two o'clock. No sign of the bug. Ticking intermittent. Wife fast asleep.*

"*Three o'clock. No sign of the bug. Ticking pretty steady. Julia and Anna getting sleepy.*

"*Four o'clock. No sign of the bug. Ticking regular, but not spirited. Wife, Julia, and Anna, all fast asleep in their chairs.*

"*Five o'clock. No sign of the bug. Ticking faint. Myself feeling drowsy. The rest still asleep.*"

So far the journal.

—Rap! rap! rap!

A terrific, portentous rapping against a door.
Startled from our dreams, we started to our feet.
Rap! rap! rap!
Julia and Anna shrieked.
I cowered in the corner.
"You fools!" cried my wife, "it's the baker with the bread."
Six o'clock.
She went to throw back the shutters, but ere it was done, a cry came from Julia. There, half in and half out its crack, there wriggled the bug, flashing in the room's general dimness, like a fiery opal.

Had this bug had a tiny sword by its side—a Damascus sword—and a tiny necklace round its neck—a diamond necklace—and a tiny gun in its claw—brass gun—and a tiny manuscript in its mouth—a Chaldee manuscript—Julia and Anna could not have stood more charmed.

In truth, it was a beautiful bug—a Jew jeweler's bug—a bug like a sparkle of a glorious sunset.

Julia and Anna had never dreamed of such a bug. To them, bug had been a word synonymous with hideousness. But this was a seraphical bug; or rather, all it had of the bug was the B, for it was beautiful as a butterfly.

Julia and Anna gazed and gazed. They were no more alarmed. They were delighted.

"But how got this strange, pretty creature into the table?" cried Julia.

"Spirits can get anywhere," replied Anna.

"Pshaw!" said my wife.

"Do you hear any more ticking?" said I.

They all applied their ears, but heard nothing.

"Well, then, wife and daughters, now that it is all over, this very morning I will go and make inquiries about it."

"Oh, do, papa," cried Julia, "do go and consult Madame Pazzi, the conjuress."

"Better go and consult Professor Johnson, the naturalist," said my wife.

"Bravo, Mrs. Democritus!" said I. "Professor Johnson is the man."

By good fortune I found the professor in. Informing him briefly of the incident, he manifested a cool, collected sort of interest, and gravely accompanied me home. The table was produced, the two openings pointed out, the bug displayed, and the details of the affair set forth; my wife and daughters being present.

"And now, Professor," said I, "what do you think of it?"

Putting on his spectacles, the learned professor looked hard at the table, and gently scraped with his penknife into the holes, but said nothing.

"Is it not an unusual thing, this?" anxiously asked Anna.

"Very unusual, Miss."

At which Julia and Anna exchanged significant glances.

"But is it not wonderful, very wonderful?" demanded Julia.

"Very wonderful, Miss."

My daughters exchanged still more significant glances, and Julia, emboldened, again spoke.

"And must you not admit, sir, that it is the work of—of—of sp—?"

"Spirits? No," was the crusty rejoinder.

"My daughters," said I, mildly, "you should remember that this is not Madame Pazzi, the conjuress, you put your questions to, but the eminent naturalist, Professor Johnson. And now, Professor," I added, "be pleased to explain. Enlighten our ignorance."

Without repeating all the learned gentleman said—for, indeed, though lucid, he was a little prosy—let the following summary of his explication suffice.

The incident was not wholly without example. The wood of the table was apple-tree, a sort of tree much fancied by various insects. The bugs had come from eggs laid inside the bark of the living tree in the orchard. By careful examination of the position of the hole from which the last bug had emerged, in relation to the cortical layers of the slab, and then allowing for the inch and a half along the grain, ere the bug had eaten its way entirely out, and then computing the whole number of cortical layers in the slab, with a reasonable conjecture for the number cut off from the outside, it appeared that the egg must have been laid in the tree some ninety years, more or less, before the tree could have been felled. But between the felling of the tree and the present time, how long might that be? It was a very old-fashioned table. Allow eighty years for the age of the table, which would make one hundred and fifty years that the bug had laid in the egg. Such, at least, was Professor Johnson's computation.

"Now, Julia," said I, "after that scientific statement of the case (though, I confess, I don't exactly understand it) where are your spirits? It is very wonderful as it is, but where are your spirits?"

"Where, indeed?" said my wife.

"Why, now, she did not *really* associate this purely natural phenomenon with any crude, spiritual hypothesis, did she?" observed the learned professor, with a slight sneer.

"Say what you will," said Julia, holding up, in the covered tumbler, the glorious, lustrous, flashing, live opal, "say what you will, if this beauteous creature be not a spirit, it yet teaches a spiritual lesson. For if, after one hundred and fifty years' entombment, a mere insect comes forth at last into light, itself an effulgence, shall there be no glorified resurrection for the spirit of man? Spirits! spirits!" she exclaimed, with rapture, "I still believe in them with delight, when before I but thought of them with terror."

The mysterious insect did not long enjoy its radiant life; it expired the next day. But my girls have preserved it. Embalmed in a silver vinaigrette, it lies on the little apple-tree table in the pier of the cedar-parlor.

And whatever lady doubts this story, my daughters will be happy to show her both the bug and the table, and point out to her, in the repaired slab of the latter, the two sealing-wax drops designating the exact place of the two holes made by the two bugs, something in the same way in which are marked the spots where the cannon balls struck Brattle Street church.

HAWTHORNE AND HIS MOSSES

BY A VIRGINIAN SPENDING JULY IN VERMONT

A papered chamber in a fine old farmhouse, a mile from any other dwelling, and dipped to the eaves in foliage—surrounded by mountains, old woods, and Indian pools,—this surely, is the place to write of Hawthorne. Some charm is in this northern air, for love and duty seem both impelling to the task. A man of a deep and noble nature has seized me in this seclusion. His wild, witch-voice rings through me; or, in softer cadences, I seem to hear it in the songs of the hillside birds that sing in the larch trees at my window.

Would that all excellent books were foundlings, without father or mother, that so it might be we could glorify them, without including their ostensible authors! Nor would any true man take exception to this; least of all, he who writes, "When the artist rises high enough to achieve the beautiful, the symbol by which he makes it perceptible to mortal senses becomes of little value in his eyes, while his spirit possesses itself in the enjoyment of the reality."

But more than this. I know not what would be the right name to put on the title-page of an excellent book; but this I feel, that the names of all fine authors are fictitious ones, far more so than that of Junius; simply standing, as they do, for the mystical ever-eluding spirit of all beauty, which ubiquitously possesses men of genius. Purely imaginative as this fancy may appear, it nevertheless seems to receive some warranty from the fact, that on a personal interview no great author has ever come up to the idea of his reader. But that dust of which our bodies are composed, how can it fitly express the nobler intelligences among us? With reverence be it spoken, that not even in the case of one deemed more than man, not even in our Saviour, did his visible frame betoken anything of the augustness of the nature within. Else, how could those Jewish eyewitnesses fail to see heaven in his glance!

It is curious how a man may travel along a country road, and yet miss the grandest or sweetest of prospects by reason of an intervening hedge, so like all other hedges, as in no way to hint of the wide landscape beyond. So has it been with me concerning the enchanting landscape in the soul of this Hawthorne, this most excellent Man of Mosses. His Old Manse has been written now four years, but I never read it till a day or two since. I had seen it in the book-stores—heard of it often—even had it recommended to me by a tasteful friend, as a rare, quiet book, perhaps too deserving of popularity to be popular. But there are so many books called "excellent," and so much unpopular merit, that amid the thick stir of other things, the hint of my tasteful friend was disregarded and for four years the Mosses on the Old Manse never refreshed me with their perennial green. It may be, however, that all this while the book, likewise, was only improving in flavor and body. At any rate, it so chanced that this long procrastination eventuated in a happy result. At breakfast the other day, a mountain girl, a cousin of mine, who for the last two weeks has every morning helped me to strawberries and raspberries, which, like the roses and pearls in the fairy tale, seemed to fall into the saucer from those strawberry-beds, her cheeks—this delightful creature, this charming Cherry says to me—"I see you spend your mornings in the haymow; and yesterday I found there Dwight's *Travels in New England*. Now I have something far better than that, something more congenial to our summer on these hills. Take these raspberries, and then I will give you some moss." "Moss!" said I. "Yes, and you must take it to the barn with you, and good-by to Dwight."

With that she left me, and soon returned with a volume, verdantly bound, and garnished with a curious frontispiece in green; nothing less than a fragment of real moss, cunningly pressed to a fly-leaf. "Why, this," said I, spilling my raspberries, "this is the *Mosses from an Old Manse*." "Yes," said cousin Cherry, "yes, it is that flowery Hawthorne." "Hawthorne and Mosses," said I, "no more it is morning: it is July in the country: and I am off for the barn."

Stretched on that new mown clover, the hillside breeze blowing over me through the wide barn door, and soothed by the hum of the bees in the meadows around, how magically stole over me this Mossy Man! and how amply, how bountifully, did he redeem that delicious promise to his guests in the Old Manse, of whom it is written: "Others could give them pleasure, or amusement, or instruction—these could be picked up anywhere; but it was for me to give them rest—rest, in a life of trouble! What better could be done for those weary and world-worn spirits? ... what better could be done for anybody who came within our magic circle than to throw the spell of a tranquil spirit over him?" So all that day, half-buried in the new clover, I watched this Hawthorne's "Assyrian dawn, and Paphian sunset and moonrise from the summit of our eastern hill."

The soft ravishments of the man spun me round about in a web of dreams, and when the book was closed, when the spell was over, this wizard "dismissed me with but misty reminiscences, as if I had been dreaming of him."

What a wild moonlight of contemplative humor bathes that Old Manse!—the rich and rare distilment of a spicy and slowly-oozing heart. No rollicking rudeness, no gross fun fed on fat dinners, and bred in the lees of wine,—but a humor so spiritually gentle, so high, so deep, and yet so richly relishable, that it were hardly inappropriate in an angel. It is the very religion of mirth; for nothing so human but it may be advanced to that. The orchard of the Old Manse seems the visible type of the fine mind that has described it—those twisted and contorted old trees, "they stretch out their crooked branches, and take such hold of the imagination that we remember them as humorists and odd-fellows." And then, as surrounded by these grotesque forms, and hushed in the noonday repose of this Hawthorne's spell, how aptly might the still fall of his ruddy thoughts into your soul be symbolized by: "In the stillest afternoon, if I listened, the thump of a great apple was audible, falling without a breath of wind, from the mere necessity of perfect ripeness." For no less ripe than ruddy are the apples of the thoughts and fancies in this sweet Man of Mosses.

Buds and Bird Voices. What a delicious thing is that! "Will the world ever be so decayed, that spring may not renew its greenness?" And the *Fire Worship*. Was ever the hearth so glorified into an altar before? The mere title of that piece is better than any common work in fifty folio volumes. How exquisite is this: "Nor did it lessen the charm of his soft, familiar courtesy and helpfulness that the mighty spirit, were opportunity offered him, would run riot through the peaceful house, wrap its inmates in his terrible embrace, and leave nothing of them save their whitened bones. This possibility of mad destruction only made his domestic kindness the more beautiful and touching. It was so sweet of him, being endowed with such power, to dwell day after day, and one long lonesome night after another, on the dusky hearth, only now and then betraying his wild nature by thrusting his red tongue out of the chimney-top! True, he had done much mischief in the world, and was pretty certain to do more; but his warm heart atoned for all. He was kindly to the race of man; and they pardoned his characteristic imperfections."

But he has still other apples, not quite so ruddy, though full as ripe:— apples, that have been left to wither on the tree, after the pleasant autumn gathering is past. The sketch of *The Old Apple Dealer* is conceived in the subtlest spirit of sadness; he whose "subdued and nerveless boyhood prefigured his abortive prime, which likewise contained within itself the prophecy and image of his lean and torpid age." Such touches as are in this piece cannot proceed from any common heart. They argue such a depth of tenderness, such a boundless sympathy with all forms of being, such an omnipresent love, that we must needs say that this Hawthorne is here almost alone in his generation,—at least, in the artistic manifestation of these things. Still more. Such touches as these—and many, very many similar ones, all through his chapters—furnish clues whereby we enter a little way into the intricate, profound heart where they originated. And we see that suffering, some time or other and in some shape or other,—this only can enable any man to depict it in others. All over him, Hawthorne's melancholy rests like an Indian-summer, which, though bathing a whole country in one softness, still reveals the distinctive hue of every towering hill and each far-winding vale.

But it is the least part of genius that attracts admiration. Where Hawthorne is known, he seems to be deemed a pleasant writer, with a pleasant style,—a sequestered, harmless man, from whom any deep and weighty thing would hardly be anticipated—a man who means no meanings. But there is no man, in whom humor and love, like mountain peaks, soar to such a rapt height as to receive the irradiations of the upper skies;—there is no man in whom humor and love are developed in that high form called genius; no such man can exist without also possessing, as the indispensable complement of these, a great, deep intellect, which drops down into the universe like a plummet. Or, love and humor are only the eyes through which such an intellect views this world. The great beauty in such a mind is but the product of its strength. What, to all readers, can be more charming than the piece entitled *Monsieur du Miroir*; and to a reader at all capable of fully fathoming it, what, at the same time, can possess more mystical depth of meaning?—yes, there he sits and looks at me,— this "shape of mystery," this "identical Monsieur du Miroir!" "Methinks I should tremble now were his wizard power of gliding through all impediments in search of me to place him suddenly before my eyes."

How profound, nay, appalling, is the moral evolved by the *Earth's Holocaust*; where—beginning with the hollow follies and affectations of the world,—all vanities and empty theories and forms are, one after another, and by an admirably graduated, growing comprehensiveness, thrown into the allegorical fire, till, at length, nothing is left but the all-engendering heart of man; which remaining still unconsumed, the great conflagration is naught.

Of a piece with this, is the *Intelligence Office*, a wondrous symbolizing of the secret workings in men's souls. There are other sketches still more charged with ponderous import.

The Christmas Banquet, and *The Bosom Serpent*, would be fine subjects for a curious and elaborate analysis, touching the conjectural parts of the mind that produced them. For spite of all the Indian-summer sunlight on the hither side of Hawthorne's soul, the other side—like the dark half of the physical sphere—is shrouded in a blackness, ten times black. But this darkness but gives more effect to the ever-moving dawn, that forever advances through it, and circumnavigates his world. Whether Hawthorne has simply availed himself of this mystical blackness as a means to the wondrous effects he makes it to produce in his lights and shades; or whether there really lurks in him, perhaps unknown to himself, a touch of Puritanic gloom,—this, I cannot altogether tell. Certain it is, however, that this great power of blackness in him derives its force from its appeals to that Calvinistic sense of Innate Depravity and Original Sin, from whose visitations, in some shape or other, no deeply thinking mind is always and wholly free. For, in certain moods, no man can weigh this world without throwing in something, somehow like Original Sin, to strike the uneven balance. At all events, perhaps no writer has ever wielded this terrific thought with greater terror than this same harmless Hawthorne. Still more: this black conceit pervades him through and through. You may be witched by his sunlight,—transported by the bright gildings in the skies he builds over you; but there is the blackness of darkness beyond; and even his bright gildings but fringe and play upon the edges of thunder-clouds. In one word, the world is mistaken in this Nathaniel Hawthorne. He himself must often have smiled at its absurd misconception of him. He is immeasurably deeper than the plummet of the mere critic. For it is not the brain that can test such a man; it is only the heart. You cannot come to know greatness by inspecting it; there is no glimpse to be caught of it, except by intuition; you need not ring it, you but touch it, and you find it is gold.

Now, it is that blackness in Hawthorne, of which I have spoken that so fixes and fascinates me. It may be, nevertheless, that it is too largely developed in him. Perhaps he does not give us a ray of light for every shade of his dark. But however this may be, this blackness it is that furnishes the infinite obscure of his background,—that background, against which Shakspeare plays his grandest conceits, the things that have made for

Shakspeare his loftiest but most circumscribed renown, as the profoundest of thinkers. For by philosophers Shakspeare is not adored, as the great man of tragedy and comedy:—"Off with his head; so much for Buckingham!" This sort of rant interlined by another hand, brings down the house,—those mistaken souls, who dream of Shakespeare as a mere man of Richard the Third humps and Macbeth daggers. But it is those deep far-away things in him; those occasional flashings-forth of the intuitive Truth in him; those short, quick probings at the very axis of reality;—these are the things that make Shakspeare, Shakspeare. Through the mouths of the dark characters of Hamlet, Timon, Lear, and Iago, he craftily says, or sometimes insinuates the things which we feel to be so terrifically true, that it were all but madness for any good man, in his own proper character, to utter, or even hint of them. Tormented into desperation, Lear, the frantic king, tears off the mask, and speaks the same madness of vital truth. But, as I before said, it is the least part of genius that attracts admiration. And so, much of the blind, unbridled admiration that has been heaped upon Shakspeare, has been lavished upon the least part of him. And few of his endless commentators and critics seem to have remembered, or even perceived, that the immediate products of a great mind are not so great as that undeveloped and sometimes undevelopable yet dimly-discernible greatness, to which those immediate products are but the infallible indices. In Shakspeare's tomb lies infinitely more than Shakspeare ever wrote. And if I magnify Shakspeare, it is not so much for what he did do as for what he did not do, or refrained from doing. For in this world of lies, Truth is forced to fly like a scared white doe in the woodlands; and only by cunning glimpses will she reveal herself, as in Shakspeare and other masters of the great Art of Telling the Truth,—even though it be covertly and by snatches.

But if this view of the all-popular Shakspeare be seldom taken by his readers, and if very few who extol him have ever read him deeply, or perhaps, only have seen him on the tricky stage (which alone made, and is still making him his mere mob renown)—if few men have time, or patience, or palate, for the spiritual truth as it is in that great genius—it is then no matter of surprise, that in a contemporaneous age, Nathaniel Hawthorne is a man as yet almost utterly mistaken among men. Here and there, in some quiet armchair in the noisy town, or some deep nook among the noiseless mountains, he may be appreciated for something of what he is. But unlike Shakspeare, who was forced to the contrary course by circumstances, Hawthorne (either from simple disinclination, or else from inaptitude) refrains from all the popularizing noise and show of broad farce and blood-besmeared tragedy; content with the still, rich utterance of a great intellect in repose, and which sends few thoughts into circulation, except they be arterialized at his large warm lungs, and expanded in his honest heart.

Nor need you fix upon that blackness in him, if it suit you not. Nor, indeed, will all readers discern it; for it is, mostly, insinuated to those who may best understand it, and account for it; it is not obtruded upon every one alike.

Some may start to read of Shakspeare and Hawthorne on the same page. They may say, that if an illustration were needed, a lesser light might have sufficed to elucidate this Hawthorne, this small man of yesterday. But I am not willingly one of those who, as touching Shakspeare at least, exemplify the maxim of Rochefoucauld, that "we exalt the reputation of some, in order to depress that of others";—who, to teach all noble-souled aspirants that there is no hope for them, pronounce Shakspeare absolutely unapproachable. But Shakspeare has been approached. There are minds that have gone as far as Shakspeare into the universe. And hardly a mortal man, who, at some time or other, has not felt as great thoughts in him as any you will find in Hamlet. We must not inferentially malign mankind for the sake of any one man, whoever he may be. This is too cheap a purchase of contentment for conscious mediocrity to make. Besides, this absolute and unconditional adoration of Shakspeare has grown to be a part of our Anglo-Saxon superstitions. The Thirty-Nine Articles are now Forty. Intolerance has come to exist in this matter. You must believe in Shakspeare's unapproachability, or quit the country. But what sort of a belief is this for an American, a man who is bound to carry republican progressiveness into Literature as well as into Life? Believe me, my friends, that men, not very much inferior to Shakspeare are this day being born on the banks of the Ohio. And the day will come when you shall say, Who reads a book by an Englishman that is a modern? The great mistake seems to be, that even with those Americans who look forward to the coming of a great literary genius among us, they somehow fancy he will come in the costume of Queen Elizabeth's day; be a writer of dramas founded upon old English history or the tales of Boccaccio. Whereas, great geniuses are parts of the times, they themselves are the times, and possess a corresponding coloring. It is of a piece with the Jews, who, while their Shiloh was meekly walking in their streets, were still praying for his magnificent coming; looking for him in a chariot, who was already among them on an ass. Nor must we forget that, in his own lifetime, Shakspeare was not Shakspeare, but only Master William Shakspeare of the shrewd, thriving, business firm of Condell, Shakspeare and Co., proprietors of the Globe Theatre in London; and by a courtly author, of the name of Chettle, was looked at as an "upstart crow," beautified "with other birds' feathers." For, mark it well, imitation is often the first charge brought against originality. Why this is so, there is not space to set forth here. You must have plenty of sea-room to tell the Truth in; especially when it seems to have an aspect of newness, as America did in 1492, though it was then just as old, and perhaps older than Asia, only those sagacious philosophers, the common sailors, had never seen it before, swearing it was all water and moonshine there.

Now I do not say that Nathaniel of Salem is a greater man than William of Avon, or as great. But the difference between the two men is by no means immeasurable. Not a very great deal more, and Nathaniel were verily William.

This, too, I mean, that if Shakspeare has not been equalled, give the world time, and he is sure to be surpassed in one hemisphere or the other. Nor will it at all do to say that the world is getting grey and grizzled now, and has lost that fresh charm which she wore of old, and by virtue of which the great poets of past times made themselves what we esteem them to be. Not so. The world is as young to-day as when it was created; and this Vermont morning dew is as wet to my feet, as Eden's dew to Adam's. Nor has nature been all over ransacked by our progenitors, so that no new charms and mysteries remain for this latter generation to find. Far from it. The trillionth part has not yet been said; and all that has been said, but multiplies the avenues to what remains to be said. It is not so much paucity as superabundance of material that seems to incapacitate modern authors.

Let America, then, prize and cherish her writers; yea, let her glorify them. They are not so many in number as to exhaust her goodwill. And while she has good kith and kin of her own, to take to her bosom, let her not lavish her embraces upon the household of an alien. For believe it or not, England after all, is in many things an alien to us. China has more bonds of real love for us than she. But even were there no strong literary individualities among us, as there are some dozens at least, nevertheless, let America first praise mediocrity even, in her children, before she praises (for everywhere, merit demands acknowledgment from every one) the best excellence in the children of any other land. Let her own authors, I say, have the priority of appreciation. I was much pleased with a hot-headed Carolina cousin of mine, who once said,—"If there were no other

American to stand by, in literature, why, then, I would stand by Pop Emmons and his *Fredoniad*, and till a better epic came along, swear it was not very far behind the *Iliad*." Take away the words, and in spirit he was sound.

Not that American genius needs patronage in order to expand. For that explosive sort of stuff will expand though screwed up in a vice, and burst it, though it were triple steel. It is for the nation's sake, and not for her authors' sake, that I would have America be heedful of the increasing greatness among her writers. For how great the shame, if other nations should be before her, in crowning her heroes of the pen! But this is almost the case now. American authors have received more just and discriminating praise (however loftily and ridiculously given, in certain cases) even from some Englishmen, than from their own countrymen. There are hardly five critics in America; and several of them are asleep. As for patronage, it is the American author who now patronizes his country, and not his country him. And if at times some among them appeal to the people for more recognition, it is not always with selfish motives, but patriotic ones.

It is true, that but few of them as yet have evinced that decided originality which merits great praise. But that graceful writer, who perhaps of all Americans has received the most plaudits from his own country for his productions,—that very popular and amiable writer, however good and self-reliant in many things, perhaps owes his chief reputation to the self-acknowledged imitation of a foreign model, and to the studied avoidance of all topics but smooth ones. But it is better to fail in originality, than to succeed in imitation. He who has never failed somewhere, that man cannot be great. Failure is the true test of greatness. And if it be said, that continual success is a proof that a man wisely knows his powers,—it is only to be added, that, in that case, he knows them to be small. Let us believe it, then, once for all, that there is no hope for us in these smooth, pleasing writers that know their powers. Without malice, but to speak the plain fact, they but furnish an appendix to Goldsmith, and other English authors. And we want no American Goldsmiths, nay, we want no American Miltons. It were the vilest thing you could say of a true American author, that he were an American Tompkins. Call him an American and have done, for you cannot say a nobler thing of him. But it is not meant that all American writers should studiously cleave to nationality in their writings; only this, no American writer should write like an Englishman or a Frenchman; let him write like a man, for then he will be sure to write like an American. Let us away with this leaven of literary flunkeyism towards England. If either must play the flunkey in this thing, let England do it, not us. While we are rapidly preparing for that political supremacy among the nations which prophetically awaits us at the close of the present century, in a literary point of view, we are deplorably unprepared for it; and we seem studious to remain so. Hitherto, reasons might have existed why this should be; but no good reason exists now. And all that is requisite to amendment in this matter, is simply this; that while fully acknowledging all excellence everywhere, we should refrain from unduly lauding foreign writers, and, at the same time, duty recognize the meritorious writers that are our own;—those writers who breathe that unshackled, democratic spirit of Christianity in all things, which now takes the practical lead in this world, though at the same time led by ourselves—us Americans. Let us boldly condemn all imitation, though it comes to us graceful and fragrant as the morning; and foster all originality though at first it be crabbed and ugly as our own pine knots. And if any of our authors fail, or seem to fail, then, in the words of my Carolina cousin, let us clap him on the shoulder and back him against all Europe for his second round. The truth is, that in one point of view this matter of a national literature has come to pass with us, that in some sense we must turn bullies, else the day is lost, or superiority so far beyond us, that we can hardly say it will ever be ours.

And now, my countrymen, as an excellent author of your own flesh and blood,—an unimitating, and, perhaps, in his way, an inimitable man—whom better can I commend to you, in the first place, than Nathaniel Hawthorne. He is one of the new, and far better generation of your writers. The smell of young beeches and hemlocks is upon him; your own broad prairies are in his soul; and if you travel away inland into his deep and noble nature, you will hear the far roar of his Niagara. Give not over to future generations the glad duty of acknowledging him for what he is. Take that joy to yourself, in your own generation; and so shall he feel those grateful impulses on him, that may possibly prompt him to the full flower of some still greater achievement in your eyes. And by confessing him you thereby confess others; you brace the whole brotherhood. For genius, all over the world, stands hand in hand, and one shock of recognition runs the whole circle round.

In treating of Hawthorne, or rather of Hawthorne in his writings (for I never saw the man; and in the chances of a quiet plantation life, remote from his haunts, perhaps never shall); in treating of his works, I say, I have thus far omitted all mention of his *Twice Told Tales*, and *Scarlet Letter*.

Both are excellent, but full of such manifold, strange, and diffusive beauties, that time would all but fail me to point the half of them out. But there are things in those two books, which, had they been written in England a century ago, Nathaniel Hawthorne had utterly displaced many of the bright names we now revere on authority. But I am content to leave Hawthorne to himself, and to the infallible finding of posterity; and however great may be the praise I have bestowed upon him, I feel that in so doing I have served and honored myself, than him. For, at bottom, great excellence is praise enough to itself; but the feeling of a sincere and appreciative love and admiration towards it, this is relieved by utterance, and warm, honest praise ever leaves a pleasant flavor in the mouth; and it is an honorable thing to confess to what is honorable in others.

But I cannot leave my subject yet. No man can read a fine author, and relish him to his very bones while he reads, without subsequently fancying to himself some ideal image of the man and his mind. And if you rightly look for it, you will almost always find that the author himself has somewhere furnished you with his own picture. For poets (whether in prose or verse), being painters by nature, are like their brethren of the pencil, the true portrait-painters, who, in the multitude of likenesses to be sketched, do not invariably omit their own; and in all high instances, they paint them without any vanity, though at times with a lurking something that would take several pages to properly define.

I submit it, then, to those best acquainted with the man personally, whether the following is not Nathaniel Hawthorne;—and to himself, whether something involved in it does not express the temper of his mind,—that lasting temper of all true, candid men—a seeker, not a finder yet:

A man now entered, in neglected attire, with the aspect of a thinker, but somewhat too roughhewn and brawny for a scholar. His face was full of sturdy vigor, with some finer and keener attribute beneath; though harsh at first, it was tempered with the glow of a large, warm heart, which had force enough to heat his powerful intellect through and through. He advanced to the Intelligencer, and looked at him with a glance of such stern sincerity, that perhaps few secrets were beyond its scope.

"I seek for Truth," said he.

Twenty-four hours have elapsed since writing the foregoing. I have just returned from the haymow, charged more and more with love and admiration of Hawthorne. For I have just been gleaning through the Mosses, picking up many things here and there that had previously escaped me. And I found that but to glean after this man, is better than to be in at the harvest of others. To be frank (though, perhaps, rather foolish) notwithstanding what I wrote yesterday of these Mosses, I had not then culled them all; but had, nevertheless, been sufficiently sensible of the subtle essence in them, as to write as I did. To what infinite height of loving wonder and admiration I may yet be borne, when by repeatedly banqueting on these Mosses I shall have thoroughly incorporated their whole stuff into my being—that, I cannot tell. But already I feel that this Hawthorne has dropped germinous seeds into my soul. He expands and deepens down, the more I contemplate him; and further and further, shoots his strong New England roots into the hot soil in my Southern soul.

By careful reference to the table of contents, I now find that I have gone through all the sketches; but that when I yesterday wrote, I had not at all read two particular pieces, to which I now desire to call special attention—*A Select Party* and *Young Goodman Brown*. Here, be it said to all those whom this poor fugitive scrawl of mine may tempt to the perusal of the Mosses, that they must on no account suffer themselves to be trifled with, disappointed, or deceived by the triviality of many of the titles to these sketches. For in more than one instance, the title utterly belies the piece. It is as if rustic demijohns containing the very best and costliest of Falernian and Tokay, were labelled "Cider," "Perry," and "Elderberry wine." The truth seems to be, that like many other geniuses, this Man of Mosses takes great delight in hoodwinking the world,—at least, with respect to himself. Personally, I doubt not that he rather prefers to be generally esteemed but a so-so sort of author; being willing to reserve the thorough and acute appreciation of what he is, to that party most qualified to judge—that is, to himself. Besides, at the bottom of their natures, men like Hawthorne, in many things, deem the plaudits of the public such strong presumptive evidence of mediocrity in the object of them, that it would in some degree render them doubtful of their own powers, did they hear much and vociferous braying concerning them in the public pastures. True, I have been braying myself (if you please to be witty enough to have it so), but then I claim to be the first that has so brayed in this particular matter; and, therefore, while pleading guilty to the charge, still claim all the merit due to originality.

But with whatever motive, playful or profound, Nathaniel Hawthorne has chosen to entitle his pieces in the manner he has, it is certain that some of them are directly calculated to deceive—egregiously deceive, the superficial skimmer of pages. To be downright and candid once more, let me cheerfully say, that two of these titles did dolefully dupe no less an eager-eyed reader than myself; and that, too, after I had been impressed with a sense of the great depth and breadth of this American man. "Who in the name of thunder" (as the country people say in this neighborhood), "who in the name of thunder, would anticipate any marvel in a piece entitled *Young Goodman Brown*?" You would of course suppose that it was a simple little tale, intended as a supplement to *Goody Two Shoes*. Whereas, it is deep as Dante; nor can you finish it, without addressing the author in his own words—"It shall be yours to penetrate, in every bosom, the deep mystery of sin".... And with Young Goodman, too, in allegorical pursuit of his Puritan wife, you cry out in your anguish:

"Faith!" shouted Goodman Brown, in a voice of agony and desperation; and the echoes of the forest mocked him, crying, "Faith! Faith!" as if bewildered wretches were seeking her all through the wilderness.

Now this same piece entitled *Young Goodman Brown*, is one of the two that I had not all read yesterday; and I allude to it now, because it is, in itself, such a strong positive illustration of the blackness in Hawthorne, which I had assumed from the mere occasional shadows of it; as revealed in several of the other sketches. But had I previously perused *Young Goodman Brown*, I should have been at no pains to draw the conclusion, which I came to at a time when I was ignorant that the book contained one such direct and unqualified manifestation of it.

The other piece of the two referred to, is entitled *A Select Party*, which, in my first simplicity upon originally taking hold of the book, I fancied must treat of some pumpkin-pie party in old Salem; or some chowder party on Cape Cod. Whereas, by all the gods of Peedee, it is the sweetest and sublimest thing that has been written since Spenser wrote. Nay, there is nothing in Spenser that surpasses it, perhaps nothing that equals it. And the test is this. Read any canto in *The Faerie Queene* and then read *A Select Party*, and decide which pleases you most,—that is, if you are qualified to judge. Do not be frightened at this; for when Spenser was alive, he was thought of very much as Hawthorne is now,—was generally accounted just such a "gentle" harmless man. It may be, that to common eyes, the sublimity of Hawthorne seems lost in his sweetness,—as perhaps in that same *Select Party* of his; for whom he has built so august a dome of sunset clouds, and served them on richer plate than Belshazzar when he banqueted his lords in Babylon.

But my chief business now, is to point out a particular page in this piece, having reference to an honored guest, who under the name of the Master Genius, but in the guise "of a young man of poor attire, with no insignia of rank or acknowledged eminence," is introduced to the Man of Fancy, who is the giver of the feast. Now, the page having reference to this Master Genius, so happily expresses much of what I yesterday wrote, touching the coming of the literary Shiloh of America, that I cannot but be charmed by the coincidence; especially, when it shows such a parity of ideas, at least in this one point, between a man like Hawthorne and a man like me.

And here, let me throw out another conceit of mine touching this American Shiloh, or Master Genius, as Hawthorne calls him. May it not be, that this commanding mind has not been, is not, and never will be, individually developed in any one man? And would it, indeed, appear so unreasonable to suppose, that this great fulness and overflowing may be, or may be destined to be, shared by a plurality of men of genius? Surely, to take the very greatest example on record, Shakspeare cannot be regarded as in himself the concretion of all the genius of his time; nor as so immeasurably beyond Marlowe, Webster, Ford, Beaumont, Jonson, that these great men can be said to share none of his power? For one, I conceive that there were dramatists in Elizabeth's day, between whom and Shakspeare the distance was by no means great. Let any one, hitherto little acquainted with those neglected old authors, for the first time read them thoroughly, or even read Charles Lamb's *Specimens* of them, and he will be amazed at the wondrous ability of those Anaks of men, and shocked at this renewed example of the fact, that Fortune has more to do with fame than merit,—though, without merit, lasting fame there can be none.

Nevertheless, it would argue too ill of my country were this maxim to hold good concerning Nathaniel Hawthorne, a man, who already, in some few minds has shed "such a light as never illuminates the earth save when a great heart burns as the household fire of a grand intellect."

The words are his,—in the *Select Party*; and they are a magnificent setting to a coincident sentiment of my own, but ramblingly expressed yesterday, in reference to himself. Gainsay it who will, as I now write, I am Posterity speaking by proxy—and after times will make it more than good, when I declare, that the American, who up to the present day has evinced, in literature, the largest brain with the largest heart, that man is Nathaniel Hawthorne. Moreover, that whatever Nathaniel Hawthorne may hereafter write, *Mosses from an Old Manse* will be ultimately accounted his masterpiece. For there is a sure, though secret sign in some works which proves the culmination of the powers (only the developable ones, however) that produced them. But I am by no means desirous of the glory of a prophet. I pray Heaven that Hawthorne may yet prove me an impostor in this prediction. Especially, as I somehow cling to the strange fancy, that, in all men, hiddenly reside certain wondrous, occult properties—as in some plants and minerals—which by some happy but very rare accident (as bronze was discovered by the melting of the iron and brass at the burning of Corinth) may chance to be called forth here on earth; not entirely waiting for their better discovery in the more congenial, blessed atmosphere of heaven.

Once more—for it is hard to be finite upon an infinite subject, and all subjects are infinite. By some people this entire scrawl of mine may be esteemed altogether unnecessary, inasmuch "as years ago" (they may say) "we found out the rich and rare stuff in this Hawthorne, who you now parade forth, as if only you *yourself* were the discoverer of this Portuguese diamond in your literature." But even granting all this—and adding to it, the assumption that the books of Hawthorne have sold by the five thousand,—what does that signify? They should be sold by the hundred thousand; and read by the million; and admired by every one who is capable of admiration.

JIMMY ROSE

A time ago, no matter how long precisely, I, an old man, removed from the country to the city, having become unexpected heir to a great old house in a narrow street of one of the lower wards, once the haunt of style and fashion, full of gay parlors and bridal chambers, but now, for the most part, transformed into counting-rooms and warehouses. There bales and boxes usurp the place of sofas; daybooks and ledgers are spread where once the delicious breakfast toast was buttered. In those old wards the glorious old soft-warfle days are over.

Nevertheless, in this old house of mine, so strangely spared, some monument of departed days survived. Nor was this the only one. Amidst the warehouse ranges some few other dwellings likewise stood. The street's transmutation was not yet complete. Like those old English friars and nuns, long haunting the ruins of their retreats after they had been despoiled, so some few strange old gentlemen and ladies still lingered in the neighborhood, and would not, could not, might not quit it. And I thought that when, one spring, emerging from my white-blossoming orchard, my own white hairs and white ivory-headed cane were added to their loitering census, that those poor old souls insanely fancied the ward was looking up—the tide of fashion setting back again.

For many years the old house had been occupied by an owner; those into whose hands it from time to time had passed having let it out to various shifting tenants; decayed old townspeople, mysterious recluses, or transient, ambiguous-looking foreigners.

While from certain cheap furbishings to which the exterior had been subjected, such as removing a fine old pulpit-like porch crowning the summit of six lofty steps, and set off with a broad-brimmed sounding-board overshadowing the whole, as well as replacing the original heavy window shutters (each pierced with a crescent in the upper panel to admit an Oriental and moony light into the otherwise shut-up rooms of a sultry morning in July) with frippery Venetian blinds; while, I repeat, the front of the house hereby presented an incongruous aspect, as if the graft of modernness had not taken in its ancient stock; still, however it might fare without, within little or nothing had been altered. The cellars were full of great grim, arched bins of blackened brick, looking like the ancient tombs of Templars, while overhead were shown the first-floor timbers, huge, square, and massive, all red oak, and through long eld, of a rich and Indian color. So large were those timbers, and so thickly ranked, that to walk in those capacious cellars was much like walking along a line-of-battle ship's gun-deck.

All the rooms in each story remained just as they stood ninety years ago with all their heavy-moulded, wooden cornices, paneled wainscots, and carved and inaccessible mantels of queer horticultural and zoological devices. Dim with longevity, the very covering of the walls still preserved the patterns of the times of Louis XVI. In the largest parlor (the drawing-room, my daughters called it, in distinction from two smaller parlors, though I did not think the distinction indispensable) the paper hangings were in the most gaudy style. Instantly we knew such paper could only have come from Paris—genuine Versailles paper—the sort of paper that might have hung in Marie Antoinette's boudoir. It was of great diamond lozenges, divided by massive festoons of roses (onions, Biddy the girl said they were, but my wife soon changed Biddy's mind on that head); and in those lozenges, one and all, as in an over-arbored garden-cage, sat a grand series of gorgeous illustrations of the natural history of the most imposing Parisian-looking birds; parrots, macaws, and peacocks, but mostly peacocks. Real Prince Esterhazies of birds; all rubies, diamonds and Orders of the Golden Fleece. But, alas! the north side of this old apartment presented a strange look; half mossy and half mildew; something as ancient forest trees on their north sides, to which particular side the moss most clings, and where, they say, internal decay first strikes. In short, the original resplendence of the peacocks had been sadly dimmed on that north side of the room, owing to a small leak in the eaves, from which the rain had slowly trickled its way down the wall, clean down to the first floor. This leak the irreverent tenants, at that period occupying the premises, did not see fit to stop, or rather, did not think it worth their while, seeing that they only kept their fuel and dried their clothes in the parlor of the peacocks. Hence many of the glowing birds seemed as if they had their princely plumage bedraggled in a dusty shower. Most mournfully their starry trains were blurred. Yet so patiently and so pleasantly, nay, here and there so ruddily did they seem to hide their bitter doom, so much of real elegance still lingered in their shapes, and so full, too, seemed they of a sweet engaging pensiveness, meditating all day long, for years and years, among their faded bowers, that though my family repeatedly adjured me (especially my wife, who, I fear, was too young for me) to destroy the whole hen-roost, as Biddy called it, and cover the walls with a beautiful, nice, genteel, cream-colored paper, despite all entreaties, I could not be prevailed upon, however submissive in other things.

But chiefly would I permit no violation of the old parlor of the peacocks or room of roses (I call it by both names) on account of its long association in my mind with one of the original proprietors of the mansion—the gentle Jimmy Rose.

Poor Jimmy Rose!

He was among my earliest acquaintances. It is not many years since he died; and I and two other tottering old fellows took hack, and in sole procession followed him to his grave.

Jimmy was born a man of moderate fortune. In his prime he had an uncommonly handsome person; large and manly, with bright eyes of blue, brown curling hair, and cheeks that seemed painted with carmine; but it was health's genuine bloom, deepened by the joy of life. He was by nature a great ladies' man, and like most deep adorers of the sex, never tied up his freedom of general worship by making one willful sacrifice of himself at the altar.

Adding to his fortune by a large and princely business, something like that of the great Florentine trader, Cosmo the Magnificent, he was enabled to entertain on a grand scale. For a long time his dinners, suppers and balls, were not to be surpassed by any given in the party-giving city of New York. His uncommon cheeriness; the splendor of his dress; his sparkling wit; radiant chandeliers; infinite fund of small-talk; French furniture; glowing welcomes to his guests; his bounteous heart and board; his noble graces and his glorious wine; what wonder if all these drew crowds to Jimmy's hospitable abode? In the winter assemblies he figured first on the manager's list. James Rose, Esq., too, was the man to be found foremost in all presentations of plate to highly successful actors at the Park, or of swords and guns to highly successful generals in the field. Often, also, was he chosen to present the gift on account of his fine gift of finely saying fine things.

"Sir," said he, in a great drawing-room in Broadway, as he extended toward General G— a brace of pistols set with turquoise, "Sir," said Jimmy with a Castilian flourish and a rosy smile, "there would have been more turquoise here set, had the names of your glorious victories left room."

Ah, Jimmy, Jimmy! Thou didst excel in compliments. But it was inwrought with thy inmost texture to be affluent in all things which give pleasure. And who shall reproach thee with borrowed wit on this occasion, though borrowed indeed it was? Plagiarize otherwise as they may, not often are the men of this world plagiarists in praise.

But times changed. Time, true plagiarist of the seasons.

Sudden and terrible reverses in business were made mortal by mad prodigality on all hands. When his affairs came to be scrutinized, it was found that Jimmy could not pay more than fifteen shillings in the pound. And yet in time the deficiency might have been made up—of course, leaving Jimmy penniless—had it not been that in one winter gale two vessels of his from China perished off Sandy Hook; perished at the threshold of their port.

Jimmy was a ruined man.

It was years ago. At that period I resided in the country, but happened to be in the city on one of my annual visits. It was but four or five days since seeing Jimmy at his house the centre of all eyes, and hearing him at the close of the entertainment toasted by a brocaded lady, in these well-remembered words: "Our noble host; the bloom on his cheek, may it last long as the bloom in his heart!" And they, the sweet ladies and gentlemen there, they drank that toast so gayly and frankly off; and Jimmy, such a kind, proud, grateful tear stood in his honest eye, angelically glancing round at the sparkling faces, and equally sparkling, and equally feeling, decanters.

Ah! poor, poor Jimmy—God guard us all—poor Jimmy Rose!

Well, it was but four or five days after this that I heard a clap of thunder—no, a clap of bad news. I was crossing the Bowling Green in a snow-storm not far from Jimmy's house on the Battery, when I saw a gentleman come sauntering along, whom I remembered at Jimmy's table as having been the first to spring to his feet in eager response to the lady's toast. Not more brimming the wine in his lifted glass than the moisture in his eye on that happy occasion.

Well, this good gentleman came sailing across the Bowling Green, swinging a silver-headed rattan; seeing me, he paused: "Ah, lad, that was rare wine Jimmy gave us the other night. Sha'n't get any more, though. Heard the news? Jimmy's burst. Clean smash, I assure you. Come along down to the Coffeehouse and I'll tell you more. And if you say so, we'll arrange over a bottle of claret for a sleighing party to Cato's to-night. Come along."

"Thank you," said I, "I—I—I am engaged."

Straight as an arrow I went to Jimmy's. Upon inquiring for him, the man at the door told me that his master was not in; nor did he know where he was; nor had his master been in the house for forty-eight hours.

Walking up Broadway again, I questioned passing acquaintances; but though each man verified the report, no man could tell where Jimmy was, and no one seemed to care, until I encountered a merchant, who hinted that probably Jimmy, having scraped up from the wreck a snug lump of coin, had prudently betaken himself off to parts unknown. The next man I saw, a great nabob he was too, foamed at the mouth when I mentioned Jimmy's name. "Rascal; regular scamp, Sir, is Jimmy Rose! But there are keen fellows after him." I afterward heard that this indignant gentleman had lost the sum of seventy-five dollars and seventy-five cents indirectly through Jimmy's failure. And yet I dare say the share of the dinners he had eaten at Jimmy's might more than have balanced that sum, considering that he was something of a wine-bibber, and such wines as Jimmy imported cost a plum or two. Indeed, now that I bethink me, I recall how I had more than once observed this same middle-aged gentleman, and how that toward the close of one of Jimmy's dinners he would sit at the table pretending to be earnestly talking with beaming Jimmy, but all the while, with a half furtive sort of tremulous eagerness and hastiness, pour down glass after glass of noble wine, as if now, while Jimmy's bounteous sun was at meridian, was the time to make his selfish hay.

At last I met a person famed for his peculiar knowledge of whatever was secret or withdrawn in the histories and habits of noted people. When I inquired of this person where Jimmy could possibly be, he took me close to Trinity Church rail, out of the jostling of the crowd, and whispered me, that Jimmy had the evening before entered an old house of his (Jimmy's), in C— Street, which old house had been for a time untenanted. The inference seemed to be that perhaps Jimmy might be lurking there now. So getting the precise locality, I bent my steps in that direction, and at last halted before the house containing the room of roses. The shutters were closed, and cobwebs were spun in their crescents. The whole place had a dreary, deserted air. The snow lay unswept, drifted in one billowed heap against the porch, no footprint tracking it. Whoever was within, surely that lonely man was an abandoned one. Few or no people were in the street; for even at that period one fashion of the street had departed from it, while trade had not as yet occupied what its rival had renounced.

Looking up and down the sidewalk a moment, I softly knocked at the door. No response. I knocked again, and louder. No one came. I knocked and rung both; still without effect. In despair I was going to quit the spot, when, as a last resource, I gave a prolonged summons, with my utmost strength, upon the heavy knocker, and then again stood still; while from various strange old windows up and down the street, various strange old heads were thrust out in wonder at so clamorous a stranger. As if now frightened from its silence, a hollow, husky voice addressed me through the keyhole.

"Who are you?" it said.

"A friend."

"Then shall you not come in," replied the voice, more hollowly than before.

Great heavens! this is not Jimmy Rose, thought I, starting. This is the wrong house. I have been misdirected. But still, to make all sure, I spoke again.

"Is James Rose within there?"

No reply.

Once more I spoke:

"I am William Ford; let me in."

"Oh, I can not, I can not! I am afraid of every one."

It *was* Jimmy Rose!

"Let me in, Rose; let me in, man. I am your friend."

"I will not. I can trust no man now."

"Let me in, Rose; trust at least one, in me."

"Quit the spot, or—"

With that I heard a rattling against the huge lock, not made by any key, as if some small tube were being thrust into the keyhole. Horrified, I fled fast as feet could carry me.

I was a young man then, and Jimmy was not more than forty. It was five-and-twenty years ere I saw him again. And what a change. He whom I expected to behold—if behold at all—dry, shrunken, meagre, cadaverously fierce with misery and misanthropy—amazement! the old Persian roses bloomed in his cheeks. And yet poor as any rat; poor in the last dregs of poverty; a pauper beyond almshouse pauperism; a promenading pauper in a thin, threadbare, careful coat; a pauper with wealth of polished words; a courteous, smiling, shivering gentleman.

Ah, poor, poor Jimmy—God guard us all—poor Jimmy Rose!

Though at the first onset of his calamity, when creditors, once fast friends, pursued him as carrion for jails; though then, to avoid their hunt, as well as the human eye, he had gone and denned in the old abandoned house; and there, in his loneliness, had been driven half mad, yet time and tide had soothed him down to sanity. Perhaps at bottom Jimmy was too thoroughly good and kind to be made from any cause a man-hater. And doubtless it at last seemed irreligious to Jimmy even to shun mankind.

Sometimes sweet sense of duty will entice one to bitter doom. For what could be more bitter now, in abject need, to be seen of those—nay, crawl and visit them in an humble sort, and be tolerated as an old eccentric, wandering in their parlors—who once had known him richest of the rich, and gayest of the gay? Yet this Jimmy did. Without rudely breaking him right down to it, fate slowly bent him more and more to the lowest deep. From an unknown quarter he received an income of some seventy dollars, more or less. The principal he would never touch, but, by various modes of eking it out, managed to live on the interest. He lived in an attic, where he supplied himself with food. He took but one regular repast a day—meal and milk—and nothing more, unless procured at others' tables. Often about the tea-hour he would drop in upon some old acquaintance, clad in his neat, forlorn frock coat, with worn velvet sewed upon the edges of the cuffs, and a similar device upon the hems of his pantaloons, to hide that dire look of having been grated off by rats. On Sunday he made a point of always dining at some fine house or other.

It is evident that no man could with impunity be allowed to lead this life unless regarded as one who, free from vice, was by fortune brought so low that the plummet of pity alone could reach him. Not much merit redounded to his entertainers because they did not thrust the starving gentleman forth when he came for his alms of tea and toast. Some merit had been theirs had they clubbed together and provided him, at small cost enough, with a sufficient income to make him, in point of necessaries, independent of the daily dole of charity; charity not sent to him either, but charity for which he had to trudge round to their doors.

But the most touching thing of all were those roses in his cheeks; those ruddy roses in his nipping winter. How they bloomed; whether meal or milk, and tea and toast could keep them flourishing; whether now he painted them; by what strange magic they were made to blossom so; no son of man might tell. But there they bloomed. And besides the roses, Jimmy was rich in smiles. He smiled ever. The lordly door which received him to his eleemosynary teas, know no such smiling guest as Jimmy. In his prosperous days the smile of Jimmy was famous far and wide. It should have been trebly famous now.

Wherever he went to tea, he had all of the news of the town to tell. By frequenting the reading-rooms, as one privileged through harmlessness, he kept himself informed of European affairs and the last literature, foreign and domestic. And of this, when encouragement was given, he would largely talk. But encouragement was not always given. At certain houses, and not a few, Jimmy would drop in about ten minutes before the tea-hour, and drop out again about ten minutes after it; well knowing that his further presence was not indispensable to the contentment or felicity of his host.

How forlorn it was to see him so heartily drinking the generous tea, cup after cup, and eating the flavorous bread and butter, piece after piece, when, owing to the lateness of the dinner hour with the rest, and the abundance of that one grand meal with them, no one besides Jimmy touched the bread and butter, or exceeded a single cup of Souchong. And knowing all this very well, poor Jimmy would try to hide his hunger, and yet gratify it too, by striving hard to carry on a sprightly conversation with his hostess, and throwing in the eagerest mouthfuls with a sort of absent-minded air, as if he ate merely for custom's sake, and not starvation's.

Poor, poor Jimmy—God guard us all—poor Jimmy Rose!

Neither did Jimmy give up his courtly ways. Whenever there were ladies at the table, sure were they of some fine word; though, indeed, toward the close of Jimmy's life, the young ladies rather thought his compliments somewhat musty, smacking of cocked hats and small clothes—nay, of old pawnbrokers' shoulder-lace and sword belts. For there still lingered in Jimmy's address a subdued sort of martial air; he having in his palmy days been, among other things, a general of the State militia. There seems a fatality in these militia generalships. Alas! I can recall more than two or three gentlemen who from militia generals became paupers. I am afraid to think why this is so. Is it that this military learning in a man of an unmilitary heart—that is, a gentle, peaceable heart—is an indication of some weak love of vain display? But ten to one it is not so. At any rate, it is unhandsome, if not unchristian, in the happy, too much to moralize on those who are not so.

So numerous were the houses that Jimmy visited, or so cautious was he in timing his less welcome calls, that at certain mansions he only dropped in about once a year or so. And annually upon seeing at that house the blooming Miss Frances or Miss Arabella, he would profoundly bow in his forlorn old coat, and with his soft, white hand take hers in gallant-wise, saying, "Ah, Miss Arabella, these jewels here are bright upon these fingers; but brighter would they look were it not for those still brighter diamonds of your eyes!"

Though in thy own need thou hadst no pence to give the poor, thou, Jimmy, still hadst alms to give the rich. For not the beggar chattering at the corner pines more after bread than the vain heart after compliment. The rich in their craving glut, as the poor in their craving want, we have with us always. So, I suppose, thought Jimmy Rose.

But all women are not vain, or if a little grain that way inclined, more than redeem it all with goodness. Such was the sweet girl that closed poor Jimmy's eyes. The only daughter of an opulent alderman, she knew Jimmy well, and saw to him in his declining days. During his last sickness, with her own hands she carried him jellies and blanc-mange; made tea for him in his attic, and turned the poor old gentleman in his bed. And well hadst thou deserved it, Jimmy, at that fair creature's hands; well merited to have the old eyes closed by woman's fairy fingers, who through life, in riches and in poverty, was still woman's sworn champion and devotee.

I hardly know that I should mention here one little incident connected with this young lady's ministrations, and poor Jimmy's reception of them. But it is harm to neither; I will tell it.

Chancing to be in town, and hearing of Jimmy's illness, I went to see him. And there in his lone attic I found the lovely ministrant. Withdrawing upon seeing another visitor, she left me alone with him. She had brought some little delicacies, and also several books, of such a sort as are sent by serious-minded well-wishers to invalids in a serious crisis. Now whether it was repugnance at being considered next door to death, or whether it was but the natural peevishment brought on by the general misery of his state; however it was, as the gentle girl withdrew, Jimmy, with what small remains of strength were his, pitched the books into the furthest corner, murmuring, "Why will she bring me this sad old stuff? Does she take me for a pauper? Thinks she to salve a gentleman's heart with Poor Man's Plaster?"

Poor, poor Jimmy—God guard us all—poor Jimmy Rose!

Well, well, I am an old man, and I suppose these tears I drop are dribblets from my dotage. But Heaven be praised, Jimmy needs no man's pity now.

Jimmy Rose is dead!

Meantime, as I sit within the parlor of the peacocks—that chamber from which his husky voice had come ere threatening me with the pistol— I still must meditate upon his strange example, whereof the marvel is, how after that gay, dashing, nobleman's career, he could be content to crawl through life, and peep about the marbles and mahoganies for contumelious tea and toast, where once like a very Warwick he had feasted the huzzaing world with Burgundy and venison.

And every time I look at the wilted resplendence of those proud peacocks on the wall, I bethink me of the withering change in Jimmy's once resplendent pride of state. But still again, every time I gaze upon those festoons of perpetual roses, mid which the faded peacocks hang, I bethink me of those undying roses which bloomed in ruined Jimmy's cheek.

Transplanted to another soil, all the unkind past forgot, God grant that Jimmy's roses may immortally survive!

I AND MY CHIMNEY

I and my chimney, two grey-headed old smokers, reside in the country. We are, I may say, old settlers here; particularly my old chimney, which settles more and more every day.

Though I always say, *I and my chimney*, as Cardinal Wolsey used to say, "*I and my King*," yet this egotistic way of speaking, wherein I take precedence of my chimney, is hereby borne out by the facts; in everything, except the above phrase, my chimney taking precedence of me.

Within thirty feet of the turf-sided road, my chimney—a huge, corpulent old Harry VIII of a chimney—rises full in front of me and all my possessions. Standing well up a hillside, my chimney, like Lord Rosse's monster telescope, swung vertical to hit the meridian moon, is the first object to greet the approaching traveler's eye, nor is it the last which the sun salutes. My chimney, too, is before me in receiving the first-fruits of the seasons. The snow is on its head ere on my hat; and every spring, as in a hollow beech tree, the first swallows build their nests in it.

But it is within doors that the pre-eminence of my chimney is most manifest. When in the rear room, set apart for that object, I stand to receive my guests (who, by the way call more, I suspect, to see my chimney than me) I then stand, not so much before, as, strictly speaking, behind my chimney, which is, indeed, the true host. Not that I demur. In the presence of my betters, I hope I know my place.

From this habitual precedence of my chimney over me, some even think that I have got into a sad rearward way altogether; in short, from standing behind my old-fashioned chimney so much, I have got to be quite behind the age too, as well as running behindhand in everything else. But to tell the truth, I never was a very forward old fellow, nor what my farming neighbors call a forehanded one. Indeed, those rumors about my behindhandedness are so far correct, that I have an odd sauntering way with me sometimes of going about with my hands behind my back. As for my belonging to the rear-guard in general, certain it is, I bring up the rear of my chimney—which, by the way, is this moment before me—and that, too, both in fancy and fact. In brief, my chimney is my superior; my superior by I know not how many heads and shoulders; my superior, too, in that humbly bowing over with shovel and tongs, I much minister to it; yet never does it minister, or incline over to me; but, if anything, in its settlings, rather leans the other way.

My chimney is grand seignior here—the one great domineering object, not more of the landscape, than of the house; all the rest of which house, in each architectural arrangement, as may shortly appear, is, in the most marked manner, accommodated, not to my wants, but to my chimney's, which, among other things, has the centre of the house to himself, leaving but the odd holes and corners to me.

But I and my chimney must explain; and as we are both rather obese, we may have to expatiate.

In those houses which are strictly double houses—that is, where the hall is in the middle—the fireplaces usually are on opposite sides; so that while one member of the household is wanning himself at a fire built into a recess of the north wall, say another member, the former's own brother, perhaps, may be holding his feet to the blaze before a hearth in the south wall—the two thus fairly sitting back to back. Is this well? Be it put to any man who has a proper fraternal feeling. Has it not a sort of sulky appearance? But very probably this style of chimney building originated with some architect afflicted with a quarrelsome family.

Then again, almost every modern fireplace has its separate flue—separate throughout, from hearth to chimney-top. At least such an arrangement is deemed desirable. Does not this look egotistical, selfish? But still more, all these separate flues, instead of having independent masonry establishments of their own, or instead of being grouped together in one federal stock in the middle of the house—instead of this, I say, each flue is surreptitiously honeycombed into the walls; so that these last are here and there, or indeed almost anywhere, treacherously hollow, and, in consequence, more or less weak. Of course, the main reason of this style of chimney building is to economize room. In cities, where lots are sold by the inch, small space is to spare for a chimney constructed on magnanimous principles; and, as with most thin men, who are generally tall, so with such houses, what is lacking in breadth, must be made up in height. This remark holds true even with regard to many very stylish abodes, built by the most stylish of gentlemen. And yet, when that stylish gentleman, Louis le Grand of France, would build a palace for his lady friend, Madame de Maintenon, he built it but one story high—in fact in the cottage style. But then, how uncommonly quadrangular, spacious, and broad—horizontal acres, not vertical ones. Such is the palace, which, in all its one-storied magnificence of Languedoc marble, in the garden of Versailles, still remains to this day. Any man can buy a square foot of land

and plant a liberty-pole on it; but it takes a king to set apart whole acres for a grand triannon.

But nowadays it is different; and furthermore, what originated in a necessity has been mounted into a vaunt. In towns there is large rivalry in building tall houses. If one gentleman builds his house four stories high, and another gentleman comes next door and builds five stories high, then the former, not to be looked down upon that way, immediately sends for his architect and claps a fifth and a sixth story on top of his previous four. And, not till the gentleman has achieved his aspiration, not till he has stolen over the way by twilight and observed how his sixth story soars beyond his neighbor's fifth—not till then does he retire to his rest with satisfaction.

Such folks, it seems to me, need mountains for neighbors, to take this emulous conceit of soaring out of them.

If, considering that mine is a very wide house, and by no means lofty, aught in the above may appear like interested pleading, as if I did but fold myself about in the cloak of a general proposition, cunningly to tickle my individual vanity beneath it, such misconception must vanish upon my frankly conceding, that land adjoining my alder swamp was sold last month for ten dollars an acre, and thought a rash purchase at that; so that for wide houses hereabouts there is plenty of room, and cheap. Indeed so cheap—dirt cheap—is the soil, that our elms thrust out their roots in it, and hang their great boughs over it, in the most lavish and reckless way. Almost all our crops, too, are sown broadcast, even peas and turnips. A farmer among us, who should go about his twenty-acre field, poking his finger into it here and there, and dropping down a mustard seed, would be thought a penurious, narrow-minded husbandman. The dandelions in the river-meadows, and the forget-me-nots along the mountain roads, you see at once they are put to no economy in space. Some seasons, too, our rye comes up here and there a spear, sole and single like a church-spire. It doesn't care to crowd itself where it knows there is such a deal of room. The world is wide, the world is all before us, says the rye. Weeds, too, it is amazing how they spread. No such thing as arresting them—some of our pastures being a sort of Alsatia for the weeds. As for the grass, every spring it is like Kossuth's rising of what he calls the peoples. Mountains, too, a regular camp-meeting of them. For the same reason, the same all-sufficiency of room, our shadows march and countermarch, going through their various drills and masterly evolutions, like the old imperial guard on the Champs de Mars. As for the hills, especially where the roads cross them the supervisors of our various towns have given notice to all concerned, that they can come and dig them down and cart them off, and never a cent to pay, no more than for the privilege of picking blackberries. The stranger who is buried here, what liberal-hearted landed proprietor among us grudges him six feet of rocky pasture?

Nevertheless, cheap, after all, as our land is, and much as it is trodden under foot, I, for one, am proud of it for what it bears; and chiefly for its three great lions—the Great Oak, Ogg Mountain, and my chimney.

Most houses, here, are but one and a half stories high; few exceed two. That in which I and my chimney dwell, is in width nearly twice its height, from sill to eaves—which accounts for the magnitude of its main content—besides showing that in this house, as in this country at large, there is abundance of space, and to spare, for both of us.

The frame of the old house is of wood—which but the more sets forth the solidity of the chimney, which is of brick. And as the great wrought nails, binding the clapboards, are unknown in these degenerate days, so are the huge bricks in the chimney walls. The architect of the chimney must have had the pyramid of Cheops before him; for, after that famous structure, it seems modeled, only its rate of decrease towards the summit is considerably less, and it is truncated. From the exact middle of the mansion it soars from the cellar, right up through each successive floor, till, four feet square, it breaks water from the ridge-pole of the roof, like an anvil-headed whale, through the crest of a billow. Most people, though, liken it, in that part, to a razed observatory, masoned up.

The reason for its peculiar appearance above the roof touches upon rather delicate ground. How shall I reveal that, forasmuch as many years ago the original gable roof of the old house had become very leaky, a temporary proprietor hired a band of woodmen, with their huge, cross-cut saws, and went to sawing the old gable roof clean off. Off it went, with all its birds' nests, and dormer windows. It was replaced with a modern roof, more fit for a railway wood-house than an old country gentleman's abode. This operation—razeeing the structure some fifteen feet—was, in effect upon the chimney, something like the falling of the great spring tides. It left uncommon low water all about the chimney—to abate which appearance, the same person now proceeds to slice fifteen feet off the chimney itself, actually beheading my royal old chimney—a regicidal act, which, were it not for the palliating fact that he was a poulterer by trade, and, therefore, hardened to such neck-wringings, should send that former proprietor down to posterity in the same cart with Cromwell.

Owing to its pyramidal shape, the reduction of the chimney inordinately widened its razeed summit. Inordinately, I say, but only in the estimation of such as have no eye to the picturesque. What care I, if, unaware that my chimney, as a free citizen of this free land, stands upon an independent basis of its own, people passing it, wonder how such a brick-kiln, as they call it, is supported upon mere joists and rafters? What care I? I will give a traveler a cup of switchel, if he want it; but am I bound to supply him with a sweet taste? Men of cultivated minds see, in my old house and chimney, a goodly old elephant-and-castle.

All feeling hearts will sympathize with me in what I am now about to add. The surgical operation, above referred to, necessarily brought into the open air a part of the chimney previously under cover, and intended to remain so, and, therefore, not built of what are called weather-bricks. In consequence, the chimney, though of a vigorous constitution, suffered not a little, from so naked an exposure; and, unable to acclimate itself, ere long began to fail—showing blotchy symptoms akin to those in measles. Whereupon travelers, passing my way, would wag their heads, laughing; "See that wax nose—how it melts off!" But what cared I? The same travelers would travel across the sea to view Kenilworth peeling away, and for a very good reason: that of all artists of the picturesque, decay wears the palm—I would say, the ivy. In fact, I've often thought that the proper place for my old chimney is ivied old England.

In vain my wife—with what probable ulterior intent will, ere long, appear—solemnly warned me, that unless something were done, and speedily, we should be burnt to the ground, owing to the holes crumbling through the aforesaid blotchy parts, where the chimney joined the roof. "Wife," said I, "far better that my house should burn down, than that my chimney should be pulled down, though but a few feet. They call it a wax nose; very good; not for me to tweak the nose of my superior." But at last the man who has a mortgage on the house dropped me a note, reminding me that, if my chimney was allowed to stand in that invalid condition, my policy of insurance would be void. This was a sort of hint not to be neglected. All the world over, the picturesque yields to the pocketesque. The mortgagor cared not, but the mortgagee did.

So another operation was performed. The wax nose was taken off, and a new one fitted on. Unfortunately for the expression—being put up by a squint-eyed mason, who, at the time, had a bad stitch in the same side—the new nose stands a little awry, in the same direction.

Of one thing, however, I am proud. The horizontal dimensions of the new part are unreduced.

Large as the chimney appears upon the roof, that is nothing to its spaciousness below. At its base in the cellar, it is precisely twelve feet square; and hence covers precisely one hundred and forty-four superficial feet. What an appropriation of terra firma for a chimney, and what a huge load for this earth! In fact, it was only because I and my chimney formed no part of his ancient burden, that that stout peddler, Atlas of old, was enabled to stand up so bravely under his pack. The dimensions given may, perhaps, seem fabulous. But, like those stones at Gilgal, which Joshua set up for a memorial of having passed over Jordan, does not my chimney remain, even unto this day?

Very often I go down into my cellar, and attentively survey that vast square of masonry. I stand long, and ponder over, and wonder at it. It has a druidical look, away down in the umbrageous cellar there whose numerous vaulted passages, and far glens of gloom, resemble the dark, damp depths of primeval woods. So strongly did this conceit steal over me, so deeply was I penetrated with wonder at the chimney, that one day—when I was a little out of my mind, I now think—getting a spade from the garden, I set to work, digging round the foundation, especially at the corners thereof, obscurely prompted by dreams of striking upon some old, earthen-worn memorial of that by-gone day, when, into all this gloom, the light of heaven entered, as the masons laid the foundation-stones, peradventure sweltering under an August sun, or pelted by a March storm. Plying my blunted spade, how vexed was I by that ungracious interruption of a neighbor who, calling to see me upon some business, and being informed that I was below said I need not be troubled to come up, but he would go down to me; and so, without ceremony, and without my having been forewarned, suddenly discovered me, digging in my cellar.

"Gold digging, sir?"

"Nay, sir," answered I, starting, "I was merely—ahem!—merely—I say I was merely digging—round my chimney."

"Ah, loosening the soil, to make it grow. Your chimney, sir, you regard as too small, I suppose; needing further development, especially at the top?"

"Sir!" said I, throwing down the spade, "do not be personal. I and my chimney—"

"Personal?"

"Sir, I look upon this chimney less as a pile of masonry than as a personage. It is the king of the house. I am but a suffered and inferior subject."

In fact, I would permit no gibes to be cast at either myself or my chimney; and never again did my visitor refer to it in my hearing, without coupling some compliment with the mention. It well deserves a respectful consideration. There it stands, solitary and alone—not a council—of ten flues, but, like his sacred majesty of Russia, a unit of an autocrat.

Even to me, its dimensions, at times, seem incredible. It does not look so big—no, not even in the cellar. By the mere eye, its magnitude can be but imperfectly comprehended, because only one side can be received at one time; and said side can only present twelve feet, linear measure. But then, each other side also is twelve feet long; and the whole obviously forms a square and twelve times twelve is one hundred and forty-four. And so, an adequate conception of the magnitude of this chimney is only to be got at by a sort of process in the higher mathematics by a method somewhat akin to those whereby the surprising distances of fixed stars are computed.

It need hardly be said, that the walls of my house are entirely free from fireplaces. These all congregate in the middle—in the one grand central chimney, upon all four sides of which are hearths—two tiers of hearths—so that when, in the various chambers, my family and guests are warming themselves of a cold winter's night, just before retiring, then, though at the time they may not be thinking so, all their faces mutually look towards each other, yea, all their feet point to one centre; and, when they go to sleep in their beds, they all sleep round one warm chimney, like so many Iroquois Indians, in the woods, round their one heap of embers. And just as the Indians' fire serves, not only to keep them comfortable, but also to keep off wolves, and other savage monsters, so my chimney, by its obvious smoke at top, keeps off prowling burglars from the towns—for what burglar or murderer would dare break into an abode from whose chimney issues such a continual smoke—betokening that if the inmates are not stirring, at least fires are, and in case of an alarm, candles may readily be lighted, to say nothing of muskets.

But stately as is the chimney—yea, grand high altar as it is, right worthy for the celebration of high mass before the Pope of Rome, and all his cardinals—yet what is there perfect in this world? Caius Julius Caesar, had he not been so inordinately great, they say that Brutus, Cassius, Antony, and the rest, had been greater. My chimney, were it not so mighty in its magnitude, my chambers had been larger. How often has my wife ruefully told me, that my chimney, like the English aristocracy, casts a contracting shade all round it. She avers that endless domestic inconveniences arise—more particularly from the chimney's stubborn central locality. The grand objection with her is, that it stands midway in the place where a fine entrance-hall ought to be. In truth, there is no hall whatever to the house—nothing but a sort of square landing-place, as you enter from the wide front door. A roomy enough landing-place, I admit, but not attaining to the dignity of a hall. Now, as the front door is precisely in the middle of the front of the house, inwards it faces the chimney. In fact, the opposite wall of the landing-place is formed solely by the chimney; and hence—owing to the gradual tapering of the chimney—is a little less than twelve feet in width. Climbing the chimney in this part, is the principal staircase—which, by three abrupt turns, and three minor landing-places, mounts to the second floor, where, over the front door, runs a sort of narrow gallery, something less than twelve feet long, leading to chambers on either hand. This gallery, of course, is railed; and so, looking down upon the stairs, and all those landing-places together, with the main one at bottom, resembles not a little a balcony for musicians, in some jolly old abode, in times Elizabethan. Shall I tell a weakness? I cherish the cobwebs there, and many a time arrest Biddy in the act of brushing them with her broom, and have many a quarrel with my wife and daughters about it.

Now the ceiling, so to speak, of the place where you enter the house, that ceiling is, in fact, the ceiling of the second floor, not the first. The two floors are made one here; so that ascending this turning stairs, you seem going up into a kind of soaring tower, or lighthouse. At the second landing, midway up the chimney, is a mysterious door, entering to a mysterious closet; and here I keep mysterious cordials, of a choice, mysterious flavor, made so by the constant nurturing and subtle ripening of the chimney's gentle heat, distilled through that warm mass of masonry. Better for wines is it than voyages to the Indias; my chimney itself a tropic. A chair by my chimney in a November day is as good for an invalid as a long season spent in Cuba. Often I think how grapes might ripen against my chimney. How my wife's geraniums bud there! Bud in December. Her eggs, too—can't keep them near the chimney, on account of the hatching. Ah, a warm heart has my chimney.

How often my wife was at me about that projected grand entrance-hall of hers, which was to be knocked clean through the chimney, from one end of the house to the other, and astonish all guests by its generous amplitude.

"But, wife," said I, "the chimney—consider the chimney: if you demolish the foundation, what is to support the superstructure?" "Oh, that will rest on the second floor." The truth is, women know next to nothing about the realities of architecture. However, my wife still talked of running her entries and partitions. She spent many long nights elaborating her plans; in imagination building her boasted hall through the chimney, as though its high mightiness were a mere spear of sorrel-top. At last, I gently reminded her that, little as she might fancy it, the chimney was a fact—a sober, substantial fact, which, in all her plannings, it would be well to take into full consideration. But this was not of much avail.

And here, respectfully craving her permission, I must say a few words about this enterprising wife of mine. Though in years nearly old as myself, in spirit she is young as my little sorrel mare, Trigger, that threw me last fall. What is extraordinary, though she comes of a rheumatic family, she is straight as a pine, never has any aches; while for me with the sciatica, I am sometimes as crippled up as any old apple-tree. But she has not so much as a toothache. As for her hearing—let me enter the house in my dusty boots, and she away up in the attic. And for her sight—Biddy, the housemaid, tells other people's housemaids, that her mistress will spy a spot on the dresser straight through the pewter platter, put up on purpose to hide it. Her faculties are alert as her limbs and her senses. No danger of my spouse dying of torpor. The longest night in the year I've known her lie awake, planning her campaign for the morrow. She is a natural projector. The maxim, "Whatever is, is right," is not hers. Her maxim is, Whatever is, is wrong; and what is more, must be altered; and what is still more, must be altered right away. Dreadful maxim for the wife of a dozy old dreamer like me, who dote on seventh days as days of rest, and out of a sabbatical horror of industry, will, on a week day, go out of my road a quarter of a mile, to avoid the sight of a man at work.

That matches are made in heaven, may be, but my wife would have been just the wife for Peter the Great, or Peter the Piper. How she would have set in order that huge littered empire of the one, and with indefatigable painstaking picked the peck of pickled peppers for the other.

But the most wonderful thing is, my wife never thinks of her end. Her youthful incredulity, as to the plain theory, and still plainer fact of death, hardly seems Christian. Advanced in years, as she knows she must be, my wife seems to think that she is to teem on, and be inexhaustible forever. She doesn't believe in old age. At that strange promise in the plain of

Mamre, my old wife, unlike old Abraham's, would not have jeeringly laughed within herself.

Judge how to me, who, sitting in the comfortable shadow of my chimney, smoking my comfortable pipe, with ashes not unwelcome at my feet, and ashes not unwelcome all but in my mouth; and who am thus in a comfortable sort of not unwelcome, though, indeed, ashy enough way, reminded of the ultimate exhaustion even of the most fiery life; judge how to me this unwarrantable vitality in my wife must come, sometimes, it is true, with a moral and a calm, but oftener with a breeze and a ruffle.

If the doctrine be true, that in wedlock contraries attract, by how cogent a fatality must I have been drawn to my wife! While spicily impatient of present and past, like a glass of ginger-beer she overflows with her schemes; and, with like energy as she puts down her foot, puts down her preserves and her pickles, and lives with them in a continual future; or ever full of expectations both from time and space, is ever restless for newspapers, and ravenous for letters. Content with the years that are gone, taking no thought for the morrow, and looking for no new thing from any person or quarter whatever, I have not a single scheme or expectation on earth, save in unequal resistance of the undue encroachment of hers.

Old myself, I take to oldness in things; for that cause mainly loving old Montague, and old cheese, and old wine; and eschewing young people, hot rolls, new books, and early potatoes and very fond of my old claw-footed chair, and old club-footed Deacon White, my neighbor, and that still nigher old neighbor, my betwisted old grape-vine, that of a summer evening leans in his elbow for cosy company at my window-sill, while I, within doors, lean over mine to meet his; and above all, high above all, am fond of my high-mantled old chimney. But she, out of the infatuate juvenility of hers, takes to nothing but newness; for that cause mainly, loving new cider in autumn, and in spring, as if she were own daughter of Nebuchadnezzar, fairly raving after all sorts of salads and spinages, and more particularly green cucumbers (though all the time nature rebukes such unsuitable young hankerings in so elderly a person, by never permitting such things to agree with her), and has an itch after recently-discovered fine prospects (so no graveyard be in the background), and also after Swedenborganism, and the Spirit Rapping philosophy, with other new views, alike in things natural and unnatural; and immortally hopeful, is forever making new flower-beds even on the north side of the house, where the bleak mountain wind would scarce allow the wiry weed called hard-hack to gain a thorough footing; and on the road-side sets out mere pipe-stems of young elms; though there is no hope of any shade from them, except over the ruins of her great granddaughter's gravestones; and won't wear caps, but plaits her gray hair; and takes the Ladies' Magazine for the fashions; and always buys her new almanac a month before the new year; and rises at dawn; and to the warmest sunset turns a cold shoulder; and still goes on at odd hours with her new course of history, and her French, and her music; and likes a young company; and offers to ride young colts; and sets out young suckers in the orchard; and has a spite against my elbowed old grape-vine, and my club-footed old neighbor, and my claw-footed old chair, and above all, high above all, would fain persecute, until death, my high-mantled old chimney. By what perverse magic, I a thousand times think, does such a very autumnal old lady have such a very vernal young soul? When I would remonstrate at times, she spins round on me with, "Oh, don't you grumble, old man (she always calls me old man), it's I, young I, that keep you from stagnating." Well, I suppose it is so. Yea, after all, these things are well ordered. My wife, as one of her poor relations, good soul, intimates, is the salt of the earth, and none the less the salt of my sea, which otherwise were unwholesome. She is its monsoon, too, blowing a brisk gale over it, in the one steady direction of my chimney.

Not insensible of her superior energies, my wife has frequently made me propositions to take upon herself all the responsibilities of my affairs. She is desirous that, domestically, I should abdicate; that, renouncing further rule, like the venerable Charles V, I should retire into some sort of monastery. But indeed, the chimney excepted, I have little authority to lay down. By my wife's ingenious application of the principle that certain things belong of right to female jurisdiction, I find myself, through my easy compliances, insensibly stripped by degrees of one masculine prerogative after another. In a dream I go about my fields, a sort of lazy, happy-go-lucky, good-for-nothing, loafing old Lear. Only by some sudden revelation am I reminded who is over me; as year before last, one day seeing in one corner of the premises fresh deposits of mysterious boards and timbers, the oddity of the incident at length begat serious meditation. "Wife," said I, "whose boards and timbers are those I see near the orchard there? Do you know anything about them, wife? Who put them there? You know I do not like the neighbors to use my land that way; they should ask permission first."

She regarded me with a pitying smile.

"Why, old man, don't you know I am building a new barn? Didn't you know that, old man?"

This is the poor old lady who was accusing me of tyrannizing over her.

To return now to the chimney. Upon being assured of the futility of her proposed hall, so long as the obstacle remained, for a time my wife was for a modified project. But I could never exactly comprehend it. As far as I could see through it, it seemed to involve the general idea of a sort of irregular archway, or elbowed tunnel, which was to penetrate the chimney at some convenient point under the staircase, and carefully avoiding dangerous contact with the fireplaces, and particularly steering clear of the great interior flue, was to conduct the enterprising traveler from the front door all the way into the dining-room in the remote rear of the mansion. Doubtless it was a bold stroke of genius, that plan of hers, and so was Nero's when he schemed his grand canal through the Isthmus of Corinth. Nor will I take oath, that, had her project been accomplished, then, by help of lights hung at judicious intervals through the tunnel, some Belzoni or other might have succeeded in future ages in penetrating through the masonry, and actually emerging into the dining-room, and once there, it would have been inhospitable treatment of such a traveler to have denied him a recruiting meal.

But my bustling wife did not restrict her objections, nor in the end confine her proposed alterations to the first floor. Her ambition was of the mounting order. She ascended with her schemes to the second floor, and so to the attic. Perhaps there was some small ground for her discontent with things as they were. The truth is, there was no regular passage-way up-stairs or down, unless we again except that little orchestra-gallery before mentioned. And all this was owing to the chimney, which my gamesome spouse seemed despitefully to regard as the bully of the house. On all its four sides, nearly all the chambers sidled up to the chimney for the benefit of a fireplace. The chimney would not go to them; they must needs go to it. The consequence was, almost every room, like a philosophical system, was in itself an entry, or passage-way to other rooms, and systems of rooms—a whole suite of entries, in fact. Going through the house, you seem to be forever going somewhere, and getting nowhere. It is like losing one's self in the woods; round and round the chimney you go, and if you arrive at all, it is just where you started, and so you begin again, and again get nowhere. Indeed—though I say it not in the way of fault-finding at all—never was there so labyrinthine an abode. Guests will tarry with me several weeks and every now and then, be anew astonished at some unforseen apartment.

The puzzling nature of the mansion, resulting from the chimney, is peculiarly noticeable in the dining-room, which has no less than nine doors, opening in all directions, and into all sorts of places. A stranger for the first time entering this dining-room, and naturally taking no special heed at which door he entered, will, upon rising to depart, commit the strangest blunders. Such, for instance, as opening the first door that comes handy, and finding himself stealing up-stairs by the back passage. Shutting that he will proceed to another, and be aghast at the cellar yawning at his feet. Trying a third, he surprises the housemaid at her work. In the end, no more relying on his own unaided efforts, he procures a trusty guide in some passing person, and in good time successfully emerges. Perhaps as curious a blunder as any, was that of a certain stylish young gentleman, a great exquisite, in whose judicious eyes my daughter Anna had found especial favor. He called upon the young lady one evening, and found her alone in the dining-room at her needlework. He stayed rather late; and after abundance of superfine discourse, all the while retaining his hat and cane, made his profuse adieus, and with repeated graceful bows proceeded to depart, after fashion of courtiers from the Queen, and by so doing, opening a door at random, with one hand placed behind, very effectually succeeded in backing himself into a dark pantry, where he carefully shut himself up, wondering there was no light in the entry. After several strange noises as of a cat among the crockery, he reappeared through the same door, looking uncommonly crestfallen, and, with a deeply embarrassed air, requested my daughter to designate at which of the nine he should find exit. When the mischievous Anna told me the story, she said it was surprising how unaffected and matter-of-fact the young gentleman's manner was after his reappearance. He was more candid than ever, to be sure; having inadvertently thrust his white kids into an open drawer of Havana sugar, under the impression, probably, that being what they call "a sweet fellow," his route might possibly lie in that direction.

Another inconvenience resulting from the chimney is, the bewilderment of a guest in gaining his chamber, many strange doors lying between him and it. To direct him by fingerposts would look rather queer; and just as queer in him to be knocking at every door on his route, like London's city guest, the king, at Temple-Bar.

Now, of all these things and many, many more, my family continually complained. At last my wife came out with her sweeping proposition—in toto to abolish the chimney.

"What!" said I, "abolish the chimney? To take out the backbone of anything, wife, is a hazardous affair. Spines out of backs, and chimneys out of houses, are not to be taken like frosted lead pipes from the ground. Besides," added I, "the chimney is the one grand permanence of this abode. If undisturbed by innovators, then in future ages, when all the house shall have crumbled from it, this chimney will still survive—a Bunker Hill monument. No, no, wife, I can't abolish my backbone."

So said I then. But who is sure of himself, especially an old man, with both wife and daughters ever at his elbow and ear? In time, I was persuaded to think a little better of it; in short, to take the matter into preliminary consideration. At length it came to pass that a master-mason—a rough sort of architect—one Mr. Scribe, was summoned to a conference. I formally introduced him to my chimney. A previous introduction from my wife had introduced him to myself. He had been not a little employed by that lady, in preparing plans and estimates for some of her extensive operations in drainage. Having, with much ado, exhorted from my spouse the promise that she would leave us to an unmolested survey, I began by leading Mr. Scribe down to the root of the matter, in the cellar. Lamp in hand, I descended; for though up-stairs it was noon, below it was night.

We seemed in the pyramids; and I, with one hand holding my lamp over head, and with the other pointing out, in the obscurity, the hoar mass of the chimney, seemed some Arab guide, showing the cobwebbed mausoleum of the great god Apis.

"This is a most remarkable structure, sir," said the master-mason, after long contemplating it in silence, "a most remarkable structure, sir."

"Yes," said I complacently, "every one says so."

"But large as it appears above the roof, I would not have inferred the magnitude of this foundation, sir," eyeing it critically.

Then taking out his rule, he measured it.

"Twelve feet square; one hundred and forty-four square feet! Sir, this house would appear to have been built simply for the accommodation of your chimney."

"Yes, my chimney and me. Tell me candidly, now," I added, "would you have such a famous chimney abolished?"

"I wouldn't have it in a house of mine, sir, for a gift," was the reply. "It's a losing affair altogether, sir. Do you know, sir, that in retaining this chimney, you are losing, not only one hundred and forty-four square feet of good ground, but likewise a considerable interest upon a considerable principal?"

"How?"

"Look, sir!" said he, taking a bit of red chalk from his pocket, and figuring against a whitewashed wall, "twenty times eight is so and so; then forty-two times thirty-nine is so and so—ain't it, sir? Well, add those together, and subtract this here, then that makes so and so," still chalking away.

To be brief, after no small ciphering, Mr. Scribe informed me that my chimney contained, I am ashamed to say how many thousand and odd valuable bricks.

"No more," said I fidgeting. "Pray now, let us have a look above."

In that upper zone we made two more circumnavigations for the first and second floors. That done, we stood together at the foot of the stairway by the front door; my hand upon the knob, and Mr. Scribe hat in hand.

"Well, sir," said he, a sort of feeling his way, and, to help himself, fumbling with his hat, "well, sir, I think it can be done."

"What, pray, Mr. Scribe; *what* can be done?"

"Your chimney, sir; it can without rashness be removed, I think."

"I will think of it, too, Mr. Scribe," said I, turning the knob and bowing him towards the open space without, "I will *think* of it, sir; it demands consideration; much obliged to ye; good morning, Mr. Scribe."

"It is all arranged, then," cried my wife with great glee, bursting from the nighest room.

"When will they begin?" demanded my daughter Julia.

"To-morrow?" asked Anna.

"Patience, patience, my dears," said I, "such a big chimney is not to be abolished in a minute."

Next morning it began again.

"You remember the chimney," said my wife.

"Wife," said I, "it is never out of my house and never out of my mind."

"But when is Mr. Scribe to begin to pull it down?" asked Anna.

"Not to-day, Anna," said I.

"*When*, then?" demanded Julia, in alarm.

Now, if this chimney of mine was, for size, a sort of belfry, for ding-donging at me about it, my wife and daughters were a sort of bells, always chiming together, or taking up each other's melodies at every pause, my wife the key-clapper of all. A very sweet ringing, and pealing, and chiming, I confess; but then, the most silvery of bells may, sometimes, dismally toll, as well as merrily play. And as touching the subject in question, it became so now. Perceiving a strange relapse of opposition in me, wife and daughters began a soft and dirge-like, melancholy tolling over it.

At length my wife, getting much excited, declared to me, with pointed finger, that so long as that chimney stood, she should regard it as the monument of what she called my broken pledge. But finding this did not answer, the next day, she gave me to understand that either she or the chimney must quit the house.

Finding matters coming to such a pass, I and my pipe philosophized over them awhile, and finally concluded between us, that little as our hearts went with the plan, yet for peace' sake, I might write out the chimney's death-warrant, and, while my hand was in, scratch a note to Mr. Scribe.

Considering that I, and my chimney, and my pipe, from having been so much together, were three great cronies, the facility with which my pipe consented to a project so fatal to the goodliest of our trio; or rather, the way in which I and my pipe, in secret, conspired together, as it were, against our unsuspicious old comrade—this may seem rather strange, if not suggestive of sad reflections upon us two. But, indeed, we, sons of clay, that is my pipe and I, are no whit better than the rest. Far from us, indeed, to have volunteered the betrayal of our crony. We are of a peaceable nature, too. But that love of peace it was which made us false to a mutual friend, as soon as his cause demanded a vigorous vindication. But, I rejoice to add, that better and braver thoughts soon returned, as will now briefly be set forth.

To my note, Mr. Scribe replied in person.

Once more we made a survey, mainly now with a view to a pecuniary estimate.

"I will do it for five hundred dollars," said Mr. Scribe at last, again hat in hand.

"Very well, Mr. Scribe, I will think of it," replied I, again bowing him to the door.

Not unvexed by this, for the second time, unexpected response, again he withdrew, and from my wife, and daughters again burst the old exclamations.

The truth is, resolved how I would, at the last pinch I and my chimney could not be parted.

"So Holofernes will have his way, never mind whose heart breaks for it," said my wife next morning, at breakfast, in that half-didactic, half-reproachful way of hers, which is harder to bear than her most energetic assault. Holofernes, too, is with her a pet name for any fell domestic despot. So, whenever, against her most ambitious innovations, those which saw me quite across the grain, I, as in the present instance, stand with however little steadfastness on the defence, she is sure to call me Holofernes, and ten to one takes the first opportunity to read aloud, with a suppressed emphasis, of an evening, the first newspaper paragraph about some tyrannic day-laborer, who, after being for many years the Caligula of his family, ends by beating his long-suffering spouse to death, with a garret door wrenched off its hinges, and then, pitching his little innocents out of the window, suicidally turns inward towards the broken wall scored with the butcher's and baker's bills, and so rushes headlong to his dreadful account.

Nevertheless, for a few days, not a little to my surprise, I heard no further reproaches. An intense calm pervaded my wife, but beneath which, as in the sea, there was no knowing what portentous movements might be going on. She frequently went abroad, and in a direction which I thought not unsuspicious; namely, in the direction of New Petra, a griffin-like house of wood and stucco, in the highest style of ornamental art, graced with four chimneys in the form of erect dragons spouting smoke from their nostrils; the elegant modern residence of Mr. Scribe, which he had built for the purpose of a standing advertisement, not more of his taste as an architect, than his solidity as a master-mason.

At last, smoking my pipe one morning, I heard a rap at the door, and my wife, with an air unusually quiet for her brought me a note. As I have no correspondents except Solomon, with whom in his sentiments, at least, I entirely correspond, the note occasioned me some little surprise, which was not dismissed upon reading the following:—

New Petra, April 1st.

Sir—During my last examination of your chimney, possibly you may have noted that I frequently applied my rule to it in a manner apparently unnecessary. Possibly, also, at the same time, you might have observed in me more or less of perplexity, to which, however, I refrained from giving any verbal expression.

I now feel it obligatory upon me to inform you of what was then but a dim suspicion, and as such would have been unwise to give utterance to, but which now, from various subsequent calculations assuming no little probability, it may be important that you should not remain in further ignorance of.

It is my solemn duty to warn you, sir, that there is architectural cause to conjecture that somewhere concealed in your chimney is a reserved space, hermetically closed, in short, a secret chamber, or rather closet. How long it has been there, it is for me impossible to say. What it contains is hid, with itself, in darkness. But probably a secret closet would not have been contrived except for some extraordinary object, whether for the concealment of treasure, or for what other purpose, may be left to those better acquainted with the history of the house to guess.

But enough: in making this disclosure, sir, my conscience is eased. Whatever step you choose to take upon it, is of course a matter of indifference to me; though, I confess, as respects the character of the closet, I cannot but share in a natural curiosity.

Trusting that you may be guided aright, in determining whether it is Christian-like knowingly to reside in a house, hidden in which is a secret closet,

> I remain,
> With much respect,
> Yours very humbly,
> Hiram Scribe.

My first thought upon reading this note was, not of the alleged mystery of manner to which, at the outset, it alluded—for none such had I at all observed in the master-mason during his surveys—but of my late kinsman, Captain Julian Dacres, long a ship-master and merchant in the Indian trade, who, about thirty years ago, and at the ripe age of ninety, died a bachelor, and in this very house, which he had built. He was supposed to have retired into this country with a large fortune. But to the general surprise, after being at great cost in building himself this mansion, he settled down into a sedate, reserved and inexpensive old age, which by the neighbors was thought all the better for his heirs: but lo! upon opening the will, his property was found to consist but of the house and grounds, and some ten thousand dollars in stocks; but the place, being found heavily mortgaged, was in consequence sold. Gossip had its day, and left the grass quietly to creep over the captain's grave, where he still slumbers in a privacy as unmolested as if the billows of the Indian Ocean, instead of the billows of inland verdure, rolled over him. Still, I remembered long ago, hearing strange solutions whispered by the country people for the mystery involving his will, and, by reflex, himself; and that, too, as well in conscience as purse. But people who could circulate the report (which they did), that Captain Julian Dacres had, in his day, been a Borneo pirate, surely were not worthy of credence in their collateral notions. It is queer what wild whimsies of rumors will, like toadstools, spring up about any eccentric stranger, who settling down among a rustic population, keeps quietly to himself. With some, inoffensiveness would seem a prime cause of offense. But what chiefly had led me to scout at these rumors, particularly as referring to concealed treasure, was the circumstance, that the stranger (the same who razeed the roof and the chimney) into whose hands the estate had passed on my kinsman's death, was of that sort of character, that had there been the least ground for those reports, he would speedily have tested them, by tearing down and rummaging the walls.

Nevertheless, the note of Mr. Scribe, so strangely recalling the memory of my kinsman, very naturally chimed in with what had been mysterious, or at least unexplained, about him; vague flashings of ingots united in my mind with vague gleamings of skulls. But the first cool thought soon dismissed such chimeras; and, with a calm smile, I turned towards my wife, who, meantime, had been sitting near by, impatient enough, I dare say, to know who could have taken it into his head to write me a letter.

"Well, old man," said she, "who is it from, and what is it about?"

"Read it, wife," said I, handing it.

Read it she did, and then—such an explosion! I will not pretend to describe her emotions, or repeat her expressions. Enough that my daughters were quickly called in to share the excitement. Although they had never dreamed of such a revelation as Mr. Scribe's; yet upon the first suggestion they instinctively saw the extreme likelihood of it. In corroboration, they cited first my kinsman, and second, my chimney; alleging that the profound mystery involving the former, and the equally profound masonry involving the latter, though both acknowledged facts, were alike preposterous on any other supposition than the secret closet.

But all this time I was quietly thinking to myself: Could it be hidden from me that my credulity in this instance would operate very favorably to a certain plan of theirs? How to get to the secret closet, or how to have any certainty about it at all, without making such fell work with my chimney as to render its set destruction superfluous? That my wife wished to get rid of the chimney, it needed no reflection to show; and that Mr. Scribe, for all his pretended disinterestedness, was not opposed to pocketing five hundred dollars by the operation, seemed equally evident. That my wife had, in secret, laid heads together with Mr. Scribe, I at present refrain from affirming. But when I consider her enmity against my chimney, and the steadiness with which at the last she is wont to carry out her schemes, if by hook or crook she can, especially after having been once baffled, why, I scarcely knew at what step of hers to be surprised.

65

Of one thing only was I resolved, that I and my chimney should not budge.

In vain all protests. Next morning I went out into the road, where I had noticed a diabolical-looking old gander, that, for its doughty exploits in the way of scratching into forbidden inclosures, had been rewarded by its master with a portentous, four-pronged, wooden decoration, in the shape of a collar of the Order of the Garotte. This gander I cornered and rummaging out its stiffest quill, plucked it, took it home, and making a stiff pen, inscribed the following stiff note:

Chimney Side, April 2.

Mr. Scribe

Sir:—For your conjecture, we return you our joint thanks and compliments, and beg leave to assure you, that
> We shall remain,
> Very faithfully,
> The same,
> I and my Chimney.

Of course, for this epistle we had to endure some pretty sharp raps. But having at last explicitly understood from me that Mr. Scribe's note had not altered my mind one jot, my wife, to move me, among other things said, that if she remembered aright, there was a statute placing the keeping in private of secret closets on the same unlawful footing with the keeping of gunpowder. But it had no effect.

A few days after, my spouse changed her key.

It was nearly midnight, and all were in bed but ourselves, who sat up, one in each chimney-corner; she, needles in hand, indefatigably knitting a sock; I, pipe in mouth, indolently weaving my vapors.

It was one of the first of the chill nights in autumn. There was a fire on the hearth, burning low. The air without was torpid and heavy; the wood, by an oversight, of the sort called soggy.

"Do look at the chimney," she began; "can't you see that something must be in it?"

"Yes, wife. Truly there is smoke in the chimney, as in Mr. Scribe's note."

"Smoke? Yes, indeed, and in my eyes, too. How you two wicked old sinners do smoke!—this wicked old chimney and you."

"Wife," said I, "I and my chimney like to have a quiet smoke together, it is true, but we don't like to be called names."

"Now, dear old man," said she, softening down, and a little shifting the subject, "when you think of that old kinsman of yours, you *know* there must be a secret closet in this chimney."

"Secret ash-hole, wife, why don't you have it? Yes, I dare say there is a secret ash-hole in the chimney; for where do all the ashes go to that drop down the queer hole yonder?"

"I know where they go to; I've been there almost as many times as the cat."

"What devil, wife, prompted you to crawl into the ash-hole? Don't you know that St. Dunstan's devil emerged from the ash-hole? You will get your death one of these days, exploring all about as you do. But supposing there be a secret closet, what then?"

"What then? why what should be in a secret closet but—"

"Dry bones, wife," broke in I with a puff, while the sociable old chimney broke in with another.

"There again! Oh, how this wretched old chimney smokes," wiping her eyes with her handkerchief. "I've no doubt the reason it smokes so is, because that secret closet interferes with the flue. Do see, too, how the jambs here keep settling; and it's down hill all the way from the door to this hearth. This horrid old chimney will fall on our heads yet; depend upon it, old man."

"Yes, wife, I do depend on it; yes indeed, I place every dependence on my chimney. As for its settling, I like it. I, too, am settling, you know, in my gait. I and my chimney are settling together, and shall keep settling, too, till, as in a great feather-bed, we shall both have settled away clean out of sight. But this secret oven; I mean, secret closet of yours, wife; where exactly do you suppose that secret closet is?"

"That is for Mr. Scribe to say."

"But suppose he cannot say exactly; what, then?"

"Why then he can prove, I am sure, that it must be somewhere or other in this horrid old chimney."

"And if he can't prove that; what, then?"

"Why then, old man," with a stately air, "I shall say little more about it."

"Agreed, wife," returned I, knocking my pipe-bowl against the jamb, "and now, to-morrow, I will for a third time send for Mr. Scribe. Wife, the sciatica takes me; be so good as to put this pipe on the mantel."

"If you get the step-ladder for me, I will. This shocking old chimney, this abominable old-fashioned old chimney's mantels are so high, I can't reach them."

No opportunity, however trivial, was overlooked for a subordinate fling at the pile.

Here, by way of introduction, it should be mentioned, that besides the fireplaces all round it, the chimney was, in the most haphazard way, excavated on each floor for certain curious out-of-the-way cupboards and closets, of all sorts and sizes, clinging here and there, like nests in the crotches of some old oak. On the second floor these closets were by far the most irregular and numerous. And yet this should hardly have been so, since the theory of the chimney was, that it pyramidically diminished as it ascended. The abridgment of its square on the roof was obvious enough; and it was supposed that the reduction must be methodically graduated from bottom to top.

"Mr. Scribe," said I when, the next day, with an eager aspect, that individual again came, "my object in sending for you this morning is, not to arrange for the demolition of my chimney, nor to have any particular conversation about it, but simply to allow you every reasonable facility for verifying, if you can, the conjecture communicated in your note."

Though in secret not a little crestfallen, it may be, by my phlegmatic reception, so different from what he had looked for; with much apparent alacrity he commenced the survey; throwing open the cupboards on the first floor, and peering into the closets on the second; measuring one within, and then comparing that measurement with the measurement without. Removing the fireboards, he would gaze up the flues. But no sign of the hidden work yet.

Now, on the second floor the rooms were the most rambling conceivable. They, as it were, dovetailed into each other. They were of all shapes; not one mathematically square room among them all—a peculiarity which by the master-mason had not been unobserved. With a significant, not to say portentous expression, he took a circuit of the chimney, measuring the area of each room around it; then going down stairs, and out of doors, he measured the entire ground area; then compared the sum total of the areas of all the rooms on the second floor with the ground area; then, returning to me in no small excitement, announced that there was a difference of no less than two hundred and odd square feet—room enough, in all conscience, for a secret closet.

"But, Mr. Scribe," said I, stroking my chin, "have you allowed for the walls, both main and sectional? They take up some space, you know."

"Ah, I had forgotten that," tapping his forehead; "but," still ciphering on his paper, "that will not make up the deficiency."

"But, Mr. Scribe, have you allowed for the recesses of so many fireplaces on a floor, and for the fire-walls, and the flues; in short, Mr. Scribe, have you allowed for the legitimate chimney itself—some one hundred and forty-four square feet or thereabouts, Mr. Scribe?"

"How unaccountable. That slipped my mind, too."

"Did it, indeed, Mr. Scribe?"

He faltered a little, and burst forth with, "But we must now allow one hundred and forty-four square feet for the legitimate chimney. My position is, that within those undue limits the secret closet is contained."

I eyed him in silence a moment; then spoke:

"Your survey is concluded, Mr. Scribe; be so good now as to lay your finger upon the exact part of the chimney wall where you believe this secret closet to be; or would a witch-hazel wand assist you, Mr. Scribe?"

"No, sir, but a crowbar would," he, with temper, rejoined.

Here, now, thought I to myself, the cat leaps out of the bag. I looked at him with a calm glance, under which he seemed somewhat uneasy. More than ever now I suspected a plot. I remembered what my wife had said about abiding by the decision of Mr. Scribe. In a bland way, I resolved to buy up the decision of Mr. Scribe.

"Sir," said I, "really, I am much obliged to you for this survey. It has quite set my mind at rest. And no doubt you, too, Mr. Scribe, must feel much relieved. Sir," I added, "you have made three visits to the chimney. With a business man, time is money. Here are fifty dollars, Mr. Scribe. Nay, take it. You have earned it. Your opinion is worth it. And by the way,"—as he modestly received the money—"have you any objections to give me a—a—little certificate—something, say, like a steamboat certificate, certifying that you, a competent surveyor, have surveyed my chimney, and found no reason to believe any unsoundness; in short, any— any secret closet in it. Would you be so kind, Mr. Scribe?"

"But, but, sir," stammered he with honest hesitation.

"Here, here are pen and paper," said I, with entire assurance.

Enough.

That evening I had the certificate framed and hung over the dining-room fireplace, trusting that the continual sight of it would forever put at rest at once the dreams and stratagems of my household.

But, no. Inveterately bent upon the extirpation of that noble old chimney, still to this day my wife goes about it, with my daughter Anna's geological hammer, tapping the wall all over, and then holding her ear against it, as I have seen the physicians of life insurance companies tap a man's chest, and then incline over for the echo. Sometimes of nights she almost frightens one, going about on this phantom errand, and still following the sepulchral response of the chimney, round and round, as if it were leading her to the threshold of the secret closet.

"How hollow it sounds," she will hollowly cry. "Yes, I declare," with an emphatic tap, "there is a secret closet here. Here, in this very spot. Hark! How hollow!"

"Psha! wife, of course it is hollow. Who ever heard of a solid chimney?" But nothing avails. And my daughters take after, not me, but their mother.

Sometimes all three abandon the theory of the secret closet and return to the genuine ground of attack—the unsightliness of so cumbrous a pile, with comments upon the great addition of room to be gained by its demolition, and the fine effect of the projected grand hall, and the convenience resulting from the collateral running in one direction and another of their various partitions. Not more ruthlessly did the Three Powers partition away poor Poland, than my wife and daughters would fain partition away my chimney.

But seeing that, despite all, I and my chimney still smoke our pipes, my wife reoccupies the ground of the secret closet, enlarging upon what wonders are there, and what a shame it is, not to seek it out and explore it.

"Wife," said I, upon one of these occasions, "why speak more of that secret closet, when there before you hangs contrary testimony of a master mason, elected by yourself to decide. Besides, even if there were a secret closet, secret it should remain, and secret it shall. Yes, wife, here for once I must say my say. Infinite sad mischief has resulted from the profane bursting open of secret recesses. Though standing in the heart of this house, though hitherto we have all nestled about it, unsuspicious of aught hidden within, this chimney may or may not have a secret closet. But if it have, it is my kinsman's. To break into that wall, would be to break into his breast. And that wall-breaking wish of Momus I account the wish of a church-robbing gossip and knave. Yes, wife, a vile eavesdropping varlet was Momus."

"Moses? Mumps? Stuff with your mumps and Moses?"

The truth is, my wife, like all the rest of the world, cares not a fig for philosophical jabber. In dearth of other philosophical companionship, I and my chimney have to smoke and philosophize together. And sitting up so late as we do at it, a mighty smoke it is that we two smoky old philosophers make.

But my spouse, who likes the smoke of my tobacco as little as she does that of the soot, carries on her war against both. I live in continual dread lest, like the golden bowl, the pipes of me and my chimney shall yet be broken. To stay that mad project of my wife's, naught answers. Or, rather, she herself is incessantly answering, incessantly besetting me with her terrible alacrity for improvement, which is a softer name for destruction. Scarce a day I do not find her with her tape-measure, measuring for her grand hall, while Anna holds a yardstick on one side, and Julia looks approvingly on from the other. Mysterious intimations appear in the nearest village paper, signed "Claude," to the effect that a certain structure, standing on a certain hill, is a sad blemish to an otherwise lovely landscape. Anonymous letters arrive, threatening me with I know not what, unless I remove my chimney. Is it my wife, too, or who, that sets up the neighbors to badgering me on the same subject, and hinting to me that my chimney, like a huge elm, absorbs all moisture from my garden? At night, also, my wife will start as from sleep, professing to hear ghostly noises from the secret closet. Assailed on all sides, and in all ways, small peace have I and my chimney.

Were it not for the baggage, we would together pack up and remove from the country.

What narrow escapes have been ours! Once I found in a drawer a whole portfolio of plans and estimates. Another time, upon returning after a day's absence, I discovered my wife standing before the chimney in earnest conversation with a person whom I at once recognized as a meddlesome architectural reformer, who, because he had no gift for putting up anything was ever intent upon pulling them down; in various parts of the country having prevailed upon half-witted old folks to destroy their old-fashioned houses, particularly the chimneys.

But worst of all was, that time I unexpectedly returned at early morning from a visit to the city, and upon approaching the house, narrowly escaped three brickbats which fell, from high aloft, at my feet. Glancing up, what was my horror to see three savages, in blue jean overalls, in the very act of commencing the long-threatened attack. Aye, indeed, thinking of those three brickbats, I and my chimney have had narrow escapes.

It is now some seven years since I have stirred from my home. My city friends all wonder why I don't come to see them, as in former times. They think I am getting sour and unsocial. Some say that I have become a sort of mossy old misanthrope, while all the time the fact is, I am simply standing guard over my mossy old chimney; for it is resolved between me and my chimney, that I and my chimney will never surrender.

THE PARADISE OF BACHELORS AND THE TARTARUS OF MAIDS

The Paradise of Bachelors

It lies not far from Temple-Bar.

Going to it, by the usual way, is like stealing from the heated plain into some cool, deep glen, shady among the harboring hills.

Sick with the din and soiled with the mud of Fleet Street—where the Benedick tradesmen are hurrying by, with ledger-lines ruled along their brows; thinking upon rise of bread and fall of babies—you adroitly turn a mystic corner—not a street—glide down a dim, monastic way, flanked by dark, sedate, and solemn piles, and still wending on, give the whole careworn world the slip, and, disentangled, stand beneath the quiet cloisters of the Paradise of Bachelors.

Sweet are the oases in Sahara; charming the isle-groves of August prairies; delectable pure faith amidst a thousand perfidies: but sweeter, still more charming, more delectable, the dreamy Paradise of Bachelors, found in the stony heart of stunning London.

In mild meditation pace the cloisters; take your pleasure, sip your leisure, in the garden waterward; go linger in the ancient library; go worship in the sculptured chapel; but little have you seen, just nothing do you know, not the kernel have you tasted, till you dine among the banded Bachelors, and see their convivial eyes and glasses sparkle. Not dine in bustling commons, during term-time, in the hall; but tranquilly, by private hint, at a private table; some fine Templar's hospitality invited guest.

Templar? That's a romantic name. Let me see. Brian de Bois Gilbert was a Templar, I believe. Do we understand you to insinuate that those famous Templars still survive in modern London? May the ring of their armed heels be heard, and the rattle of their shields, as in mailed prayer the monk-knights kneel before the consecrated Host? Surely a monk-knight were a curious sight picking his way along the Strand, his gleaming corselet and snowy surcoat spattered by an omnibus. Long-bearded, too, according to his order's rule; his face fuzzy as a pard's; how would the grim ghost look among the crop-haired, close-shaven citizens. We know indeed—sad history recounts it—that a moral blight tainted at last this sacred Brotherhood. Though no sworded foe might outskill them in the fence, yet the work of luxury crawled beneath their guard, gnawing the core of knightly troth, nibbling the monastic vows, till at last the monk's austerity relaxed to wassailing, and the sworn knights-bachelors grew to be but hypocrites and rakes.

But for all this, quite unprepared were we to learn that Knights-Templars (if at all in being) were so entirely secularized as to be reduced from carving out immortal fame in glorious battling for the Holy Land, to the carving of roast mutton at a dinner-board. Like Anacreon, do these degenerate Templars now think it sweeter far to fall in banquet hall than in war? Or, indeed, how can there be any survival of that famous order? Templars in modern London! Templars in their red-cross mantles smoking cigars at the Divan! Templars crowded in a railway train, till, stacked with steel helmet, spear, and shield, the whole train looks like one elongated locomotive!

No. The genuine Templar is long since departed. Go view the wondrous tombs in the Temple Church; see there the rigidly-haughty forms stretched out, with crossed arms upon their stilly hearts, in everlasting undreaming rest. Like the years before the flood, the bold Knights-Templars are no more. Nevertheless, the name remains, and the nominal society, and the ancient grounds, and some of the ancient edifices. But the iron heel is changed to a boot of patent-leather; the long two-handed sword to a one-handed quill; the monk-giver of gratuitous ghostly counsel now counsels for a fee; the defender of the sarcophagus (if in good practice with his weapon) now has more than one case to defend; the vowed opener and clearer of all highways leading to the Holy Sepulchre, now has it in particular charge to check, to clog, to hinder, and embarrass all the courts and avenues of Law; the Knight-combatant of the Saracen, breasting spear-point at Acre, now fights law-points in Westminster Hall. The helmet is a wig. Struck by Time's enchanter's wand, the Templar is to-day a Lawyer.

But, like many others tumbled from proud glory's height, like the apple, hard on the bough but mellow on the ground, the Templar's fall has but made him all the finer fellow.

I dare say those old warrior-priests were but gruff and grouty at the best; cased in Birmingham hardware, how could their crimped arms give yours or mine a hearty shake? Their proud, ambitious, monkish souls clasped shut, like horn-book missals; their very faces clapped in bomb-shells; what sort of genial men were these? But best of comrades, most affable of hosts, capital diner is the modern Templar. His wit and wine are both of sparkling brands.

The church and cloisters, courts and vaults, lanes and passages, banquet-halls, refectories, libraries, terraces, gardens, broad walks, domicils, and dessert-rooms, covering a very large space of ground, and all grouped in central neighborhood and quite sequestered from the old city's surrounding din; and everything about the place being kept in most bachelor-like particularity, no part of London offers a quiet wight so agreeable a refuge.

The Temple is, indeed, a city by itself. A city with all the best appurtenances, as the above enumeration shows. A city with a park to it, and flower-beds, and a riverside—the Thames flowing by as openly, in one part, as by Eden's primal garden flowed the mild Euphrates. In what is now the Temple Garden the old Crusaders used to exercise their steeds and lances; the modern Templars now lounge on the benches beneath the trees, and switching their patent-leather boots, in gay discourse exercise at repartee.

Long lines of stately portraits in the banquet-halls, show what great men of mark—famous nobles, judges, and Lord Chancellors—have in their time been Templars. But all Templars are not known to universal fame; though, if the having warm hearts and warmer welcomes, full minds and fuller cellars, and giving good advice and glorious dinners, spiced with rare divertisements of fun and fancy, merit immortal mention, set down, ye muses, the names of R.F.C. and his imperial brother.

Though to be a Templar, in the one true sense, you must needs be a lawyer, or a student at the law, and be ceremoniously enrolled as member of the order, yet as many such, though they may have their offices there, just so, on the other hand, there are many residents of the hoary old domicils who are not admitted Templars. If being, say, a lounging gentleman and bachelor, or a quiet, unmarried literary man, charmed with the soft seclusion of the spot, you much desire to pitch your shady tent among the rest in this serene encampment, then you must make some special friend among the order, and procure him to rent, in his name but at your charge, whatever vacant chamber you may find to suit.

Thus, I suppose, did Dr. Johnson, that nominal Benedick and widower but virtual bachelor, when for a space he resided here. So, too, did that undoubted bachelor and rare good soul, Charles Lamb. And hundreds more, of sterling spirits, Brethren of the Order of Celibacy, from time to time have dined, and slept, and tabernacled here. Indeed, the place is all a honeycomb of offices and domicils. Like any cheese, it is quite perforated through and through in all directions with the snug cells of bachelors. Dear, delightful spot! Ah! when I bethink me of the sweet hours there passed, enjoying such genial hospitalities beneath those time-honored roofs, my heart only finds due utterance through poetry; and, with a sigh, I softly sing, "Carry me back to old Virginny!"

Such then, at large, is the Paradise of Bachelors. And such I found it one pleasant afternoon in the smiling month of May, when, sallying from my hotel in Trafalgar Square, I went to keep my dinner-appointment with that fine Barrister, Bachelor, and Bencher, R.F.C. (he is the first and second, and should be the third; I hereby nominate him), whose card I kept fast pinched between my gloved forefinger and thumb, and every now and then snatched still another look at the pleasant address inscribed beneath the name, Number —, Elm Court, Templar.

At the core he was a right bluff, care-free, right comfortable, and most companionable Englishman. If on a first acquaintance he seemed reserved, quite icy in his air—patience; this champagne will thaw. And, if it never do, better frozen champagne than liquid vinegar.

There were nine gentlemen, all bachelors, at the dinner. One was from "Number —, King's Bench Walk, Temple"; a second, third and fourth, and fifth, from various courts or passages christened with some similarly rich resounding syllables. It was indeed a sort of Senate of the Bachelors, sent to this dinner from widely-scattered districts, to represent the general celibacy of the Temple. Nay it was, by representation, a Grand Parliament of the best Bachelors in universal London; several of those present being from distant quarters of the town, noted immemorial seats of lawyers and unmarried men—Lincoln's Inn, Furnival's Inn; and one gentlemen upon whom I looked with a sort of collateral awe, hailed from the spot where Lord Verulam once abode a bachelor—Gray's Inn.

The apartment was well up toward heaven; I know not how many strange old stairs I climbed to get to it. But a good dinner, with famous company, should be well earned. No doubt our host had his dining-room so high with a view to secure the prior exercise necessary to the due relishing and digesting of it.

The furniture was wonderfully unpretending, old, and snug. No new shining mahogany, sticky with undried varnish; no uncomfortably luxurious ottomans, and sofas too fine to use, vexed you in this sedate apartment. It is a thing which every sensible American should learn from every sensible Englishmen, that glare and glitter, gimcracks and gewgaws, are not indispensable to domestic solacement. The American Benedick snatches, down-town, a tough chop in a gilded show-box; the English bachelor leisurely dines at home on that incomparable South Down of his, off a plain deal board.

The ceiling of the room was low. Who wants to dine under the dome of St. Peter's? High ceilings! If that is your demand, and the higher the better, and you be so very tall, then go dine out with the topping giraffe in the open air.

In good time the nine gentlemen sat down to nine covers, and soon were fairly under way.

If I remember right, ox-tail soup inaugurated the affair. Of a rich russet hue, its agreeable flavor dissipated my first confounding of its main ingredient with teamster's gads and the rawhides of ushers. (By way of interlude, we here drank a little claret.) Neptune's was the next tribute rendered—turbot coming second; snow-white, flaky, and just gelatinous enough, not too turtleish in its unctuousness. (At this point we refreshed ourselves with a glass of sherry.) After these light skirmishers had vanished, the heavy artillery of the feast marched in, led by that well-known English generalissimo, roast beef. For aids-de-camp we had a saddle of mutton, a fat turkey, a chicken-pie, and endless other savory things; while for avant-couriers came nine silver flagons of humming ale. This heavy ordnance having departed on the track of the light skirmishers, a picked brigade of game-fowl encamped upon the board, their camp-fires lit by the ruddiest of decanters.

Tarts and puddings followed, with innumerable niceties; then cheese and crackers. (By way of ceremony, simply, only to keep up good old fashions, we here each drank a glass of good old port.)

The cloth was now removed; and like Blucher's army coming in at the death on the field of Waterloo, in marched a fresh detachment of bottles, dusty with their hurried march.

All these manoeuvrings of the forces were superintended by a surprising old field marshal (I can not school myself to call him by the inglorious name of waiter), with snowy hair and napkin, and a head like Socrates. Amidst all the hilarity of the feast, intent on important business, he disdained to smile. Venerable man!

I have above endeavored to give some slight schedule of the general plan of operations. But any one knows that a good, general dinner is a sort of pell-mell, indiscriminate affair, quite baffling to detail in all particulars. Thus, I spoke of taking a glass of claret, and a glass of sherry, and a glass of port, and a mug of ale—all at certain specific periods and times. But those were merely the state bumpers, so to speak. Innumerable impromptu glasses were drained between the periods of those grand imposing ones.

The nine bachelors seemed to have the most tender concern for each other's health. All the time, in flowing wine, they most earnestly expressed their sincerest wishes for the entire well-being and lasting hygiene of the gentlemen on the right and on the left. I noticed that when one of these kind bachelors desired a little more wine (just for his stomach's sake, like Timothy), he would not help himself to it unless some other bachelor would join him. It seemed held something indelicate, selfish and unfraternal to be seen taking a lonely, unparticipated glass. Meantime, as the wine ran apace, the spirits of the company grew more and more to perfect genialness and unconstraint. They related all sorts of pleasant stories. Choice experiences in their private lives were now brought out, like choice brands of Moselle or Rhenish, only kept for particular company. One told us how mellowly he lived when a student at Oxford; with various spicy anecdotes of most frank-hearted noble lords, his liberal companions. Another bachelor, a gray-headed man, with a sunny face, who, by his own account, embraced every opportunity of leisure to cross over into the Low Countries, on sudden tours of inspection of the fine old Flemish architecture there—this learned, white-haired, sunny-faced old bachelor, excelled in his descriptions of the elaborate splendors of those old guild-halls, town-halls, and stadhold-houses, to be seen in the land of the ancient Flemings. A third was a great frequenter of the British Museum, and knew all about scores of wonderful antiquities, of Oriental manuscripts, and costly books without a duplicate. A fourth had lately returned from a trip to Old Granada, and, of course, was full of Saracenic scenery. A fifth had a funny case in law to tell. A sixth was erudite in wines. A seventh had a strange characteristic anecdote of the private life of the Iron Duke, never printed, and never before announced in any public or private company. An eighth had lately been amusing his evening, now and then, with translating a comic poem of Pulci's. He quoted for us the more amusing passages.

And so the evening slipped along, the hours told, not by a water-clock, like King Alfred's but a wine-chronometer. Meantime the table seemed a sort of Epsom Heath; a regular ring, where the decanters galloped round. For fear one decanter should not with sufficient speed reach his destination, another was sent express after him to hurry him; and then a third to hurry the second; and so on with a fourth and fifth. And throughout all this nothing loud, nothing unmannerly, nothing turbulent. I am quite sure, from the scrupulous gravity and austerity of his air, that had Socrates, the field marshal, perceived aught of indecorum in the company he served, he would have forthwith departed without giving warning. I afterward learned that during the repast, an invalid bachelor in an adjoining chamber enjoyed his first sound refreshing slumber in three long weary weeks.

It was the very perfection of quiet absorption of good living, good drinking, good feeling, and good talk. We were a band of brothers. Comfort—fraternal, household comfort, was the grand trait of the affair. Also, you would plainly see that these easy-hearted men had no wives or children to give an anxious thought. Almost all of them were travelers, too; and without any twinges of their consciences touching desertion of the fireside.

The thing called pain, the bugbear styled trouble—those two legends seemed preposterous to their bachelor imaginations. How could men of liberal sense, ripe scholarship in the world, and capacious philosophical and convivial understanding—how could they suffer themselves to be imposed upon by such monkish fables? Pain! Trouble! As well talk of Catholic miracles. No such thing.—Pass the sherry, Sir.—Pooh, pooh! Can't be!—The port, Sir, if you please. Nonsense; don't tell me so.—The decanter stops with you, Sir, I believe.

And so it went.

Not long after the cloth was drawn our host glanced significantly upon Socrates, who, solemnly stepping to a stand, returned with an immense convolved horn, a regular Jericho horn, mounted with polished silver, and otherwise chased and curiously enriched; not omitting two lifelike goat's heads, with four more horns of solid silver, projecting from opposite sides of the mouth of the noble main horn.

Not having heard that our host was a performer on the bugle, I was surprised to see him lift this horn from the table, as if he were about to blow an inspiring blast. But I was relieved from this, and set quite right as touching the purposes of the horn, by his now inserting his thumb and forefinger into its mouth; whereupon a slight aroma was stirred up, and my nostrils were greeted with the smell of some choice Rappee. It was a mull of snuff. It went the rounds. Capital idea this, thought I, of taking snuff about this juncture. This goodly fashion must be introduced among my countrymen at home, further ruminated I.

The remarkable decorum of the nine bachelors—a decorum not to be affected by any quantity of wine—a decorum unassailable by any degree of mirthfulness—this was again set in a forcible light to me, by now observing that, though they took snuff very freely, yet not a man so far violated the proprieties, or so far molested the invalid bachelor in the adjoining room as to indulge himself in a sneeze. The snuff was snuffed silently, as if it had been some fine innoxious powder brushed off the wings of butterflies.

But fine though they be, bachelors' dinners, like bachelors' lives, can not endure forever. The time came for breaking up. One by one the bachelors took their hats, and two by two, and arm-in-arm they descended, still conversing, to the flagging of the court; some going to their neighboring chambers to turn over the Decameron ere retiring for the night; some to smoke a cigar, promenading in the garden on the cool riverside; some to make for the street, call a hack and be driven snugly to their distant lodgings.

I was the last lingerer.

"Well," said my smiling host, "what do you think of the Temple here, and the sort of life we bachelors make out to live in it?"

"Sir," said I, with a burst of admiring candor—"Sir, this is the very Paradise of Bachelors!"

The Tarturus of Maids

It lies not far from Woedolor Mountain in New England. Turning to the east, right out from among bright farms and sunny meadows, nodding in early June with odorous grasses, you enter ascendingly among bleak hills. These gradually close in upon a dusky pass, which, from the violent Gulf Stream of air unceasingly driving between its cloven walls of haggard rock, as well as from the tradition of a crazy spinster's hut having long ago stood somewhere hereabout, is called the Mad Maid's Bellows'-pipe.

Winding along at the bottom of the gorge is a dangerously narrow wheel-road, occupying the bed of a former torrent. Following this road to its highest point, you stand as within a Dantean gateway. From the steepness of the walls here, their strangely ebon hue, and the sudden contraction of the gorge, this particular point is called the Black Notch. The ravine now expandingly descends into a great, purple, hopper-shaped hollow, far sunk among many Plutonian, shaggy-wooded mountains. By the country people this hollow is called the Devil's Dungeon. Sounds of torrents fall on all sides upon the ear. These rapid waters unite at last in one turbid, brick-colored stream, boiling through a flume among enormous boulders. They call this strange-colored torrent Blood River. Gaining a dark precipice it wheels suddenly to the west, and makes one maniac spring of sixty feet into the arms of a stunted wood of gray-haired pines, between which it thence eddies on its further way down to the invisible lowlands.

Conspicuously crowning a rocky bluff high to one side, at the cataract's verge, is the ruin of an old saw-mill, built in those primitive times when vast pines and hemlocks superabounded throughout the neighboring region. The black-mossed bulk of those immense, rough-hewn, and spike-knotted logs, here and there tumbled all together, in long abandonment and decay, or left in solitary, perilous projection over the cataract's gloomy brink, impart to this rude wooden ruin not only much of the aspect of one of rough-quarried stone, but also a sort of feudal, Rhineland, and Thurmberg look, derived from the pinnacled wildness of the neighborhood scenery.

Not far from the bottom of the Dungeon stands a large whitewashed building, relieved, like some great white sepulchre, against the sullen background of mountain-side firs, and other hardy evergreens, inaccessibly rising in grim terraces for some two thousand feet.

The building is a paper-mill.

Having embarked on a large scale in the seedsman's business (so extensively and broadcast, indeed, that at length my seeds were distributed through all the Eastern and Northern States, and even fell into the far soil of Missouri and the Carolinas), the demand for paper at my place became so great, that the expenditure soon amounted to a most important item in the general account. It need hardly be hinted how paper comes into use with seedsmen, as envelopes. These are mostly made of yellowish paper, folded square; and when filled, are all but flat, and being stamped, and superscribed with the nature of the seeds contained, assume not a little the appearance of business letters ready for the mail. Of these small envelopes I used an incredible quantity—several hundred of thousands in a year. For a time I had purchased my paper from the wholesale dealers in a neighboring town. For economy's sake, and partly for the adventure of the trip, I now resolved to cross the mountains, some sixty miles, and order my future paper at the Devil's Dungeon paper-mill.

The sleighing being uncommonly fine toward the end of January, and promising to hold so for no small period, in spite of the bitter cold I started one gray Friday noon in my pung, well fitted with buffalo and wolf robes; and, spending one night on the road, next noon came in sight of Woedolor Mountain.

The far summit fairly smoked with frost; white vapors curled up from its white-wooded top, as from a chimney. The intense congelation made the whole country look like one petrification. The steel shoes of my pung craunched and gritted over the vitreous, chippy snow, as if it had been broken glass. The forests here and there skirting the route, feeling the same all-stiffening influence, their inmost fibres penetrated with the cold, strangely groaned—not in the swaying branches merely, but likewise in the vertical trunk—as the fitful gusts remorseless swept through them. Brittle with excessive frost, many colossal tough-grained maples, snapped in twain like pipe-stems, cumbered the unfeeling earth.

Flaked all over with frozen sweat, white as a milky ram, his nostrils at each breath sending forth two horn-shaped shoots of heated respiration, Black, my good horse, but six years old, started at a sudden turn, where, right across the track—not ten minutes fallen—an old distorted hemlock lay, darkly undulatory as an anaconda.

Gaining the Bellows'-pipe, the violent blast, dead from behind, all but shoved my high-backed pung up-hill. The gust shrieked through the shivered pass, as if laden with lost spirits bound to the unhappy world. Ere gaining the summit, Black, my horse, as if exasperated by the cutting wind, slung out with his strong hind legs, tore the light pung straight up-hill, and sweeping grazingly through the narrow notch, sped downward madly past the ruined saw-mill. Into the Devil's Dungeon horse and cataract rushed together.

With might and main, quitting my seat and robes, and standing backward, with one foot braced against the dashboard, I rasped and churned the bit, and stopped him just in time to avoid collision, at a turn, with the bleak nozzle of a rock, couchant like a lion in the way—a roadside rock.

At first I could not discover the paper-mill.

The whole hollow gleamed with the white, except, here and there, where a pinnacle of granite showed one wind-swept angle bare. The mountains stood pinned in shrouds—a pass of Alpine corpses. Where stands the mill? Suddenly a whirling, humming sound broke upon my ear. I looked, and there, like an arrested avalanche, lay the large whitewashed factory. It was subordinately surrounded by a cluster of other and smaller buildings, some of which, from their cheap, blank air, great length, gregarious windows, and comfortless expression, no doubt were boarding-houses of the operatives. A snow-white hamlet amidst the snows. Various rude, irregular squares and courts resulted from the somewhat picturesque clusterings of these buildings, owing to the broken, rocky nature of the ground, which forbade all method in their relative arrangement. Several narrow lanes and alleys, too, partly blocked with snow fallen from the roof, cut up the hamlet in all directions.

When, turning from the traveled highway, jingling with bells of numerous farmers—who, availing themselves of the fine sleighing, were dragging their wood to market—and frequently diversified with swift cutters dashing from inn to inn of the scattered villages—when, I say, turning from that bustling main-road, I by degrees wound into the Mad Maid's Bellows'-pipe, and saw the grim Black Notch beyond, then something latent, as well as something obvious in the time and scene, strangely brought back to my mind my first sight of dark and grimy Temple Bar. And when Black, my horse, went darting through the Notch, perilously grazing its rocky wall, I remembered being in a runaway London omnibus, which in much the same sort of style, though by no means at an equal rate, dashed through the ancient arch of Wren. Though the two objects did by no means correspond, yet this partial inadequacy but served to tinge the similitude not less with the vividness than the disorder of a dream. So that, when upon reining up at the protruding rock I at last caught sight of the quaint groupings of the factory-buildings, and with the traveled highway and the Notch behind, found myself all alone, silently and privily stealing through deep-cloven passages into this sequestered spot, and saw the long, high-gabled main factory edifice, with a rude tower—for hoisting heavy boxes—at one end, standing among its crowded outbuildings and boarding-houses, as the Temple Church amidst the surrounding offices and dormitories, and when the marvelous retirement of this mysterious mountain nook fastened its whole spell upon me, then, what memory lacked, all tributary imagination furnished, and I said to myself, This is the very counterpart of the Paradise of Bachelors, but snowed upon, and frost-painted in a sepulchre.

Dismounting, and warily picking my way down the dangerous declivity—horse and man both sliding now and then upon the icy ledges—at length I drove, or the blast drove me, into the largest square, before one side of the main edifice. Piercingly and shrilly the shotted blast blew by the corner; and redly and demoniacally boiled Blood River at one side. A long woodpile, of many scores of cords, all glittering in mail of crusted ice, stood crosswise in the square. A row of horse-posts, their north sides plastered with adhesive snow, flanked the factory wall. The bleak frost packed and paved the square as with some ringing metal.

The inverted similitude recurred—"The sweet, tranquil Temple garden, with the Thames bordering its green beds," strangely meditated I.

But where are the gay bachelors?

Then, as I and my horse stood shivering in the wind-spray, a girl ran from a neighboring dormitory door, and throwing her thin apron over her bare head, made for the opposite building.

"One moment, my girl; is there no shed hereabouts which I may drive into?"

Pausing, she turned upon me a face pale with work, and blue with cold; an eye supernatural with unrelated misery.

"Nay," faltered I, "I mistook you. Go on; I want nothing."

Leading my horse close to the door from which she had come, I knocked. Another pale, blue girl appeared, shivering in the doorway as, to prevent the blast, she jealously held the door ajar.

"Nay, I mistake again. In God's name shut the door. But hold, is there no man about?"

That moment a dark-complexioned well-wrapped personage passed, making for the factory door, and spying him coming, the girl rapidly closed the other one.

"Is there no horse-shed here, Sir?"

"Yonder, the wood-shed," he replied, and disappeared inside the factory.

With much ado I managed to wedge in horse and pung between scattered piles of wood all sawn and split. Then, blanketing my horse, and piling my buffalo on the blanket's top, and tucking in its edges well around the breastband and breeching, so that the wind might not strip him bare, I tied him fast, and ran lamely for the factory door, still with frost, and cumbered with my driver's dread-naught.

Immediately I found myself standing in a spacious place, intolerably lighted by long rows of windows, focusing inward the snowy scene without.

At rows of blank-looking counters sat rows of blank-looking girls, white folders in their blank hands, all blankly folding blank paper.

In one corner stood some huge frame of ponderous iron, with a vertical thing like a piston periodically rising and falling upon a heavy wooden block. Before it—its tame minister—stood a tall girl, feeding the iron animal with half-quires of rose-hued note paper, which, at every downward dab of the piston-like machine, received in the corner the impress of a wreath of roses. I looked from the rosy paper to the pallid cheek, but said nothing.

Seated before a long apparatus, strung with long, slender strings like any harp, another girl was feeding it with foolscap sheets, which, so soon as they curiously traveled from her on the cords, were withdrawn at the opposite end of the machine by a second girl. They came to the first girl blank; they went to the second girl ruled.

I looked upon the first girl's brow, and saw it was young and fair; I looked upon the the second girl's brow, and saw it was ruled and wrinkled. Then, as I still looked, the two—for some small variety to the monotony—changed places; and where had stood the young, fair brow, now stood the ruled and wrinkled one.

Perched high upon a narrow platform, and still higher upon a high stool crowning it, sat another figure serving some other iron animal; while below the platform sat her mate in some sort of reciprocal attendance.

Not a syllable was breathed. Nothing was heard but the low, steady overruling hum of the iron animals. The human voice was banished from the spot. Machinery—that vaunted slave of humanity—here stood menially served by human beings, who served mutely and cringingly as the slave serves the Sultan. The girls did not so much seem accessory wheels to the general machinery as mere cogs to the wheels.

All this scene around me was instantaneously taken in at one sweeping glance—even before I had proceeded to unwind the heavy fur tippet from around my neck. But as soon as this fell from me the dark-complexioned man, standing close by, raised a sudden cry, and seizing my arm, dragged me out into the open air, and without pausing for a word instantly caught up some congealed snow and began rubbing both my cheeks.

"Two white spots like the whites of your eyes," he said; "man, your cheeks are frozen."

"That may well be," muttered I; "'tis some wonder the frost of the Devil's Dungeon strikes in no deeper. Rub away."

Soon a horrible, tearing pain caught at my reviving cheeks. Two gaunt blood-hounds, one on either side, seemed mumbling them. I seemed Actaeon.

Presently, when all was over, I re-entered the factory, made known my business, concluded it satisfactorily, and then begged to be conducted throughout the place to view it.

"Cupid is the boy for that," said the dark-complexioned man. "Cupid!" and by this odd fancy-name calling a dimpled, red-cheeked, spirited-looking, forward little fellow, who was rather impudently, I thought, gliding about among the passive-looking girls—like a gold fish through hueless waves—yet doing nothing in particular that I could see, the man bade him lead the stranger through the edifice.

"Come first and see the water-wheel," said this lively lad, with the air of boyishly-brisk importance.

Quitting the folding-room, we crossed some damp, cold boards, and stood beneath a great wet shed, incessantly showered with foam, like the green barnacled bow of some East Indiaman in a gale. Round and round here went the enormous revolutions of the dark colossal water-wheel, grim with its one immutable purpose.

"This sets our whole machinery a-going, Sir; in every part of all these buildings; where the girls work and all."

I looked, and saw that the turbid waters of Blood River had not changed their hue by coming under the use of man.

"You make only blank paper; no printing of any sort, I suppose? All blank paper, don't you?"

"Certainly; what else should a paper-factory make?"

The lad here looked at me as if suspicious of my common-sense.

"Oh, to be sure!" said I, confused and stammering; "it only struck me as so strange that red waters should turn out pale chee—paper, I mean."

He took me up a wet and rickety stair to a great light room, furnished with no visible thing but rude, manger-like receptacles running all round its sides; and up to these mangers, like so many mares haltered to the rack stood rows of girls. Before each was vertically thrust up a long, glittering scythe, immovably fixed at bottom to the manger-edge. The curve of the scythe, and its having no snath to it, made it look exactly like a sword. To and fro, across the sharp edge, the girls forever dragged long strips of rags, washed white, picked from baskets at one side; thus ripping asunder every seam, and converting the tatters almost into lint. The air swam with the fine, poisonous particles, which from all sides darted, subtilely, as motes in sunbeams, into the lungs.

"This is the rag-room," coughed the boy.

"You find it rather stifling here," coughed I, in answer; "but the girls don't cough."

"Oh, they are used to it."

"Where do you get such hosts of rags?" picking up a handful from a basket.

"Some from the country round about; some from far over sea—Leghorn and London."

"'Tis not unlikely, then," murmured I, "that among these heaps of rags there may be some old shirts, gathered from the dormitories of the Paradise of Bachelors. But the buttons are all dropped off. Pray, my lad, do you ever find any bachelor's buttons hereabouts?"

"None grow in this part of the country. The Devil's Dungeon is no place for flowers."

"Oh! you mean the *flowers* so called—the Bachelor's Buttons?"

"And was not that what you asked about? Or did you mean the gold bosom-buttons of our boss, Old Bach, as our whispering girls all call him?"

"The man, then, I saw below is a bachelor, is he?"

"Oh, yes, he's a Bach."

"The edges of those swords, they are turned outward from the girls, if I see right; but their rags and fingers fly so, I can not distinctly see."

"Turned outward."

Yes, murmured I to myself; I see it now; turned outward; and each erected sword is so borne, edge-outward, before each girl. If my reading fails me not, just so, of old, condemned state-prisoners went from the hall of judgment to their doom; an officer before, bearing a sword, its edge turned outward, in significance of their fatal sentence. So, through consumptive pallors of this blank, raggy life, go these white girls to death.

"Those scythes look very sharp," again turning toward the boy.

"Yes; they have to keep them so. Look!"

That moment two of the girls, dropping their rags, plied each a whetstone up and down the sword-blade. My unaccustomed blood curdled at the sharp shriek of the tormented steel.

Their own executioners; themselves whetting the very swords that slay them; meditated I.

"What makes those girls so sheet-white, my lad?"

"Why"—with a roguish twinkle, pure ignorant drollery, not knowing heartlessness—"I suppose the handling of such white bits of sheets all the time makes them so sheety."

"Let us leave the rag-room now, my lad."

More tragical and more inscrutably mysterious than any mystic sight, human or machine, throughout the factory, was the strange innocence of cruel-heartedness in this usage-hardened boy.

"And now," said he, cheerily, "I suppose you want to see our great machine, which cost us twelve thousand dollars only last autumn. That's the machine that makes the paper, too. This way, Sir."

Following him I crossed a large, bespattered place, with two great round vats in it, full of a white, wet, woolly-looking stuff, not unlike the albuminous part of an egg, soft-boiled.

"There," said Cupid, tapping the vats carelessly, "these are the first beginning of the paper; this white pulp you see. Look how it swims bubbling round and round, moved by the paddle here. From hence it pours from both vats into the one common channel yonder; and so goes, mixed up and leisurely, to the great machine. And now for that."

He led me into a room, stifling with a strange, blood-like, abdominal heat, as if here, true enough, were being finally developed the germinous particles lately seen.

Before me, rolled out like some long Eastern manuscript, lay stretched one continuous length of iron framework—multitudinous and mystical, with all sorts of rollers, wheels, and cylinders, in slowly-measured and unceasing motion.

"Here first comes the pulp now," said Cupid, pointing to the nighest end of the machine.

"See; first it pours out and spreads itself upon this wide, sloping board; and then—look—slides, thin and quivering, beneath the first roller there.

Follow on now, and see it as it slides from under that to the next cylinder. There; see how it has become just a very little less pulpy now. One step more, and it grows still more to some slight consistence. Still another cylinder, and it is so knitted—though as yet mere dragon-fly wing—that it forms an air-bridge here, like a suspended cobweb, between two more separated rollers; and flowing over the last one, and under again, and doubling about there out of sight for a minute among all those mixed cylinders you indistinctly see, it reappears here, looking now at last a little less like pulp and more like paper, but still quite delicate and defective yet awhile. But—a little further onward, Sir, if you please—here now, at this further point, it puts on something of a real look, as if it might turn out to be something you might possibly handle in the end. But it's not yet done, Sir. Good way to travel yet, and plenty more of cylinders must roll it."

"Bless my soul!" said I, amazed at the elongation, interminable convolutions, and deliberate slowness of the machine. "It must take a long time for the pulp to pass from end to end, and come out paper."

"Oh, not so long," smiled the precocious lad, with a superior and patronizing air; "only nine minutes. But look; you may try it for yourself. Have you a bit of paper? Ah! here's a bit on the floor. Now mark that with any word you please, and let me dab it on here, and we'll see how long before it comes out at the other end."

"Well, let me see," said I, taking out my pencil. "Come, I'll mark it with your name."

Bidding me take out my watch, Cupid adroitly dropped the inscribed slip on an exposed part of the incipient mass.

Instantly my eye marked the second-hand on my dial-plate.

Slowly I followed the slip, inch by inch: sometimes pausing for full half a minute as it disappeared beneath inscrutable groups of the lower cylinders, but only gradually to emerge again; and so, on, and on, and on—inch by inch; now in open sight, sliding along like a freckle on the quivering sheet; and then again wholly vanished; and so, on, and on, and on—inch by inch; all the time the main sheet growing more and more to final firmness—when, suddenly, I saw a sort of paper-fall, not wholly unlike a water-fall; a scissory sound smote my ear, as of some cord being snapped; and down dropped an unfolded sheet of perfect foolscap, with my "Cupid" half faded out of it, and still moist and warm.

My travels were at an end, for here was the end of the machine.

"Well, how long was it?" said Cupid.

"Nine minutes to a second," replied I, watch in hand.

"I told you so."

For a moment a curious emotion filled me, not wholly unlike that which one might experience at the fulfillment of some mysterious prophecy. But how absurd, thought I again; the thing is a mere machine, the essence of which is unvarying punctuality and precision.

Previously absorbed by the wheels and cylinders, my attention was now directed to a sad-looking woman standing by.

"That is rather an elderly person so silently tending the machine-end here. She would not seem wholly used to it either."

"Oh," knowingly whispered Cupid, through the din, "she only came last week. She was a nurse formerly. But the business is poor in these parts, and she's left it. But look at the paper she is piling there."

"Ay, foolscap," handling the piles of moist, warm sheets, which continually were being delivered into the woman's waiting hands. "Don't you turn out anything but foolscap at this machine?"

"Oh, sometimes, but not often, we turn out finer work—cream-laid and royal sheets, we call them. But foolscap being in chief demand we turn out foolscap most."

It was very curious. Looking at that blank paper continually dropping, dropping, dropping, my mind ran on in wonderings of those strange uses to which those thousand sheets eventually would be put. All sorts of writings would be writ on those now vacant things—sermons, lawyers' briefs, physicians' prescriptions, love-letters, marriage certificates, bills of divorce, registers of births, death-warrants, and so on, without end. Then, recurring back to them as they here lay all blank, I could not but bethink me of that celebrated comparison of John Locke, who, in demonstration of his theory that man had no innate ideas, compared the human mind at birth to a sheet of blank paper, something destined to be scribbled on, but what sort of characters no soul might tell.

Pacing slowly to and fro along the involved machine, still humming with its play, I was struck as well by the inevitability as the evolvement-power in all its motions.

"Does that thin cobweb there," said I, pointing to the sheet in its more imperfect stage, "does that never tear or break? It is marvelous fragile, and yet this machine it passes through is so mighty."

"It never is known to tear a hair's point."

"Does it never stop—get clogged?"

"No. It *must* go. The machinery makes it go just *so*; just that very way, and at that very pace you there plainly *see* it go. The pulp can't help going."

Something of awe now stole over me, as I gazed upon this inflexible iron animal. Always, more or less, machinery of this ponderous elaborate sort strikes, in some moods, strange dread into the human heart, as some living, panting Behemoth might. But what made the thing I saw so specially terrible to me was the metallic necessity, the unbudging fatality which governed it. Though, here and there, I could not follow the thin, gauzy vail of pulp in the course of its more mysterious or entirely invisible advance, yet it was indubitable that, at those points where it eluded me, it still marched on in unvarying docility to the autocratic cunning of the machine. A fascination fastened on me. I stood spellbound and wandering in my soul. Before my eyes—there, passing in slow procession along the wheeling cylinders, I seemed to see, glued to the pallid incipience of the pulp, the yet more pallid faces of all the pallid girls I had eyed that heavy day. Slowly, mournfully, beseechingly, yet unresistingly, they gleamed along, their agony dimly outlined on the imperfect paper, like the print of the tormented face on the handkerchief of Saint Veronica.

"Halloa! the heat of this room is too much for you," cried Cupid, staring at me.

"No—I am rather chill, if anything."

"Come out, Sir—out—out," and, with the protecting air of a careful father, the precocious lad hurried me outside.

In a few minutes, feeling revived a little, I went into the folding-room— the first room I had entered, and where the desk for transacting business stood, surrounded by the blank counters and blank girls engaged at them.

"Cupid here has led me a strange tour," said I to the dark-complexioned man before mentioned, whom I had ere this discovered not only to be an old bachelor, but also the principal proprietor. "Yours is a most wonderful factory. Your great machine is a miracle of inscrutable intricacy."

"Yes, all our visitors think it so. But we don't have many. We are in a very out-of-the-way corner here. Few inhabitants, too. Most of our girls come from far-off villages."

"The girls," echoed I, glancing round at their silent forms. "Why is it, Sir, that in most factories, female operatives, of whatever age, are indiscriminately called girls, never women?"

"Oh! as to that—why, I suppose, the fact of their being generally unmarried—that's the reason, I should think. But it never struck me before. For our factory here, we will not have married women; they are apt to be off-and-on too much. We want none but steady workers; twelve hours to the day, day after day, through the three hundred and sixty-five days, excepting Sundays, Thanksgiving, and Fast-days. That's our rule. And so, having no married women, what females we have are rightly enough called girls."

"Then these are all maids," said I, while some pained homage to their pale virginity made me involuntarily bow.

"All maids."

Again the strange emotion filled me.

"Your cheeks look whitish yet, Sir," said the man, gazing at me narrowly. "You must be careful going home. Do they pain you at all now? It's a bad sign, if they do."

"No doubt, Sir," answered I, "when once I have got out of the Devil's Dungeon I shall feel them mending."

"Ah, yes; the winter air in valleys, or gorges, or any sunken place, is far colder and more bitter than elsewhere. You would hardly believe it now, but it is colder here than at the top of Woedolor Mountain."

"I dare say it is, Sir. But time presses me; I must depart."

With that, remuffling myself in dread-naught and tippet, thrusting my hands into my huge sealskin mittens, I sallied out into the nipping air, and found poor Black, my horse, all cringing and doubled up with the cold.

Soon, wrapped in furs and meditations, I ascended from the Devil's Dungeon.

At the Black Notch I paused, and once more bethought me of Temple-Bar. Then, shooting through the pass, all alone with inscrutable nature, I exclaimed—Oh! Paradise of Bachelors! and oh! Tartarus of Maids!

COCK-A-DOODLE-DOO!

OR THE CROWING OF THE NOBLE COCK BENEVENTANO

In all parts of the world many high-spirited revolts from rascally despotisms had of late been knocked on the head; many dreadful casualties, by locomotive and steamer, had likewise knocked hundreds of high-spirited travelers on the head (I lost a dear friend in one of them); my own private affairs were also full of despotisms, casualties, and knockings on the head, when early one morning in spring, being too full of hypoes to sleep, I sallied out to walk on my hillside pasture.

It was a cool and misty, damp, disagreeable air. The country looked underdone, its raw juices squirting out all round. I buttoned out this squitchy air as well as I could with my lean, double-breasted dress-coat—my overcoat being so long-skirted I only used it in my wagon—and spitefully thrusting my crab-stick into the oozy sod, bent my blue form to the steep ascent of the hill. This toiling posture brought my head pretty well earthward, as if I were in the act of butting it against the world. I marked the fact, but only grinned at it with a ghastly grin.

All round me were tokens of a divided empire. The old grass and the new grass were striving together. In the low wet swales the verdure peeped out in vivid green; beyond, on the mountains, lay light patches of snow, strangely relieved against their russet sides; all the humped hills looked like brindled kine in the shivers. The woods were strewn with dry dead boughs, snapped off by the riotous winds of March, while the young trees skirting the woods were just beginning to show the first yellowish tinge of the nascent spray.

I sat down for a moment on a great rotting log nigh the top of the hill, my back to a heavy grove, my face presented toward a wide sweeping circuit of mountains enclosing a rolling, diversified country. Along the base of one long range of heights ran a lagging, fever-and-agueish river, over which was a duplicate stream of dripping mist, exactly corresponding in every meander with its parent water below. Low down, here and there, shreds of vapor listlessly wandered in the air, like abandoned or helmless nations or ships—or very soaky towels hung on criss-cross clothes-lines to dry. Afar, over a distant village lying in a bay of the plain formed by the mountains, there rested a great flat canopy of haze, like a pall. It was the condensed smoke of the chimneys, with the condensed, exhaled breath of the villagers, prevented from dispersion by the imprisoning hills. It was too heavy and lifeless to mount of itself; so there it lay, between the village and the sky, doubtless hiding many a man with the mumps, and many a queasy child.

My eye ranged over the capacious rolling country, and over the mountains, and over the village, and over a farmhouse here and there, and over woods, groves, streams, rocks, fells—and I thought to myself, what a slight mark, after all, does man make on this huge great earth. Yet the earth makes a mark on him. What a horrid accident was that on the Ohio, where my good friend and thirty other good fellows were sloped into eternity at the bidding of a thick-headed engineer, who knew not a valve from a flue. And that crash on the railroad just over yon mountains there, where two infatuate trains ran pell-mell into each other, and climbed and clawed each other's backs; and one locomotive was found fairly shelled like a chick, inside of a passenger car in the antagonist train; and near a score of noble hearts, a bride and her groom, and an innocent little infant, were all disembarked into the grim hulk of Charon, who ferried them over, all baggageless, to some clinkered iron-foundry country or other. Yet what's the use of complaining? What justice of the peace will right this matter? Yea, what's the use of bothering the very heavens about it? Don't the heavens themselves ordain these things—else they could not happen?

A miserable world! Who would take the trouble to make a fortune in it, when he knows not how long he can keep it, for the thousand villains and asses who have the management of railroads and steamboats, and innumerable other vital things in the world. If they would make me Dictator in North America awhile I'd string them up! and hang, draw, and quarter; fry, roast and boil; stew, grill, and devil them like so many turkey-legs—the rascally numskulls of stokers; I'd set them to stokering in Tartarus—I would!

Great improvements of the age! What! to call the facilitation of death and murder an improvement! Who wants to travel so fast? My grandfather did not, and he was no fool. Hark! here comes that old dragon again—that gigantic gadfly of a Moloch—snort! puff! scream!—here he comes straight-bent through these vernal woods, like the Asiatic cholera cantering on a camel. Stand aside! Here he comes, the chartered murderer! the death monopolizer! judge, jury, and hangman all together, whose victims die always without benefit of clergy. For two hundred and fifty miles that iron fiend goes yelling through the land, crying "More! more! more!" Would fifty conspiring mountains fall atop of him! and, while they were about it, would they would also fall atop of that smaller dunning fiend, my creditor, who frightens the life out of me more than any locomotive—a lantern-jawed rascal, who seems to run on a railroad track too, and duns me even on Sunday, all the way to church and back, and comes and sits in the same pew with me, and pretending to be polite and hand me the prayer-book opened at the proper place, pokes his pesky bill under my nose in the very midst of my devotions, and so shoves himself between me and salvation; for how can one keep his temper on such occasions?

I can't pay this horrid man; and yet they say money was never so plentiful—a drug on the market; but blame me if I can get any of the drug, though there never was a sick man more in need of that particular sort of medicine. It's a lie; money ain't plenty—feel of my pocket. Ha! here's a powder I was going to send to the sick baby in yonder hovel, where the Irish ditcher lives. That baby has the scarlet fever. They say the measles are rife in the country too, and the varioloid, and the chicken-pox, and it's bad for teething children. And after all, I suppose many of the poor little ones, after going through all this trouble snap off short; and so they had the measles, mumps, croup, scarlet-fever, chicken-pox, cholera-morbus, summer-complaint, and all else, in vain! Ah! there's that twinge of the rheumatics in my right shoulder. I got it one night on the North River, when, in a crowded boat, I gave up my berth to a sick lady, and staid on deck till morning in drizzling weather. There's the thanks one gets for charity! Twinge! Shoot away, ye rheumatics! Ye couldn't lay on worse if I were some villain who had murdered the lady instead of befriending her. Dyspepsia too—I am troubled with that.

Hallo! here come the calves, the two-year-olds, just turned out of the barn into the pasture, after six months of cold victuals. What a miserable-looking set, to be sure! A breaking up of a hard winter, that's certain; sharp bones sticking out like elbows; all quilted with a strange stuff dried on their flanks like layers of pancakes. Hair worn quite off too, here and there; and where it ain't pancaked, or worn off, looks like the rubbed sides of mangy old hair-trunks. In fact, they are not six two-year-olds, but six abominable old hair-trunks wandering about here in this pasture.

Hark! By Jove, what's that? See! the very hair-trunks prick their ears at it, and stand and gaze away down into the rolling country yonder. Hark again! How clear! how musical! how prolonged! What a triumphant thanksgiving of a cock-crow! *"Glory be to God in the highest!"* It says those very words as plain as ever cock did in this world. Why, why, I began to feel a little in sorts again. It ain't so very misty, after all. The sun yonder is beginning to show himself; I feel warmer.

Hark! There again! Did ever such a blessed cock-crow so ring out over the earth before! Clear, shrill, full of pluck, full of fire, full of fun, full of glee. It plainly says—"*Never say die!*" My friends, it is extraordinary, is it not?

Unwittingly, I found that I had been addressing the two-year-olds—the calves—in my enthusiasm; which shows how one's true nature will betray itself at times in the most unconscious way. For what a very two-year-old, and calf, I had been to fall into the sulks, on a hilltop too, when a cock down in the lowlands there, without discourse of reason, and quite penniless in the world, and with death hanging over him at any moment from his hungry master, sends up a cry like a very laureate celebrating the glorious victory of New Orleans.

Hark! there it goes again! My friends, that must be a Shanghai; no domestic-born cock could crow in such prodigious exulting strains. Plainly, my friends, a Shanghai of the Emperor of China's breed.

But my friends the hair-trunks, fairly alarmed at last by such clamorously-victorious tones, were now scampering off, with their tails flirting in the air, and capering with their legs in clumsy enough sort of style, sufficiently evincing that they had not freely flourished them for the six months last past.

Hark! there again! Whose cock is that? Who in this region can afford to buy such an extraordinary Shanghai? Bless me—it makes my blood bound—I feel wild. What? jumping on this rotten old log here, to flap my elbows and crow too? And just now in the doleful dumps. And all this from the simple crow of a cock. Marvelous cock! But soft—this fellow now crows most lustily; but it's only morning; let's see how he'll crow about noon, and towards nightfall. Come to think of it, cocks crow most lustily in the beginning of the day. Their pluck ain't lasting, after all. Yes, yes; even cocks have to succumb to the universal spell of tribulation: jubilant in the beginning, but down in the mouth at the end.

... "*Of fine mornings, We fine lusty cocks begin our crows in gladness; But when the eve does come we don't crow quite so much, For then cometh despondency and madness.*"

The poet had this very Shanghai in mind when he wrote that. But stop. There he rings out again, ten times richer, fuller, longer, more obstreperously exulting than before! In fact, that bell ought to be taken down, and this Shanghai put in its place. Such a crow would jollify all

London, from Mile-End (which is no end) to Primrose Hill (where there ain't any primroses), and scatter the fog.

Well, I have an appetite for my breakfast this morning, if I have not had it for a week before. I meant to have only tea and toast; but I'll have coffee and eggs—no, brown stout and a beefsteak. I want something hearty. Ah, here comes the down-train: white cars, flashing through the trees like a vein of silver. How cheerfully the steam-pipe chirps! Gay are the passengers. There waves a handkerchief—going down to the city to eat oysters, and see their friends, and drop in at the circus. Look at the mist yonder; what soft curls and undulations round the hills, and the sun weaving his rays among them. See the azure smoke of the village, like the azure tester over a bridal-bed. How bright the country looks there where the river overflowed the meadows. The old grass has to knock under to the new. Well, I feel the better for this walk. Home now, and walk into that steak and crack that bottle of brown stout; and by the time that's drank—a quart of stout—by that time, I shall feel about as stout as Samson. Come to think of it, that dun may call, though. I'll just visit the woods and cut a club. I'll club him, by Jove, if he duns me this day.

Hark! there goes Shanghai again. Shanghai says, "Bravo!" Shanghai says, "Club him!"

Oh, brave cock!

I felt in rare spirits the whole morning. The dun called about eleven. I had the boy Jake send the dun up. I was reading *Tristram Shandy*, and could not go down under the circumstances. The lean rascal (a lean farmer, too—think of that!) entered, and found me seated in an armchair, with my feet on the table, and the second bottle of brown stout handy, and the book under eye.

"Sit down," said I, "I'll finish this chapter, and then attend to you. Fine morning. Ha! ha!—this is a fine joke about my Uncle Toby and the Widow Wadman! Ha! ha! ha! let me read this to you."

"I have no time; I've got my noon *chores* to do."

"To the deuce with your *chores*!" said I. "Don't drop your old tobacco about here, or I'll turn you out."

"Sir!"

"Let me read you this about the Widow Wadman. Said the Widow Wadman—"

"There's my bill, sir."

"Very good. Just twist it up, will you—it's about my smoking-time; and hand a coal, will you, from the hearth yonder!"

"My bill, sir!" said the rascal, turning pale with rage and amazement at my unwonted air (formerly I had always dodged him with a pale face), but too prudent as yet to betray the extremity of his astonishment. "My bill, sir"—and he stiffly poked it at me.

"My friend," said I, "what a charming morning! How sweet the country looks! Pray, did you hear that extraordinary cock-crow this morning? Take a glass of my stout!"

"*Yours?* First pay your debts before you offer folks *your* stout!"

"You think, then, that, properly speaking, I have no *stout*," said I, deliberately rising. "I'll undeceive you. I'll show you stout of a superior brand to Barclay and Perkins."

Without more ado, I seized that insolent dun by the slack of his coat—(and, being a lean, shad-bellied wretch, there was plenty of slack to it)—I seized him that way, tied him with a sailor-knot, and, thrusting his bill between his teeth, introduced him to the open country lying round about my place of abode.

"Jake," said I, "you'll find a sack of bluenosed potatoes lying under the shed. Drag it here, and pelt this pauper away; he's been begging pence of me, and I know he can work, but he's lazy. Pelt him away, Jake!"

Bless my stars, what a crow! Shanghai sent up such a perfect pæan and *laudamus*—such a trumpet blast of triumph, that my soul fairly snorted in me. Duns!—I could have fought an army of them! Plainly, Shanghai was of the opinion that duns only came into the world to be kicked, hanged, bruised, battered, choked, walloped, hammered, drowned, clubbed!

Returning indoors, when the exultation of my victory over the dun had a little subsided, I fell to musing over the mysterious Shanghai. I had no idea I would hear him so nigh my house. I wondered from what rich gentleman's yard he crowed. Nor had he cut short his crows so easily as I had supposed he would. This Shanghai crowed till midday, at least. Would he keep a-crowing all day? I resolved to learn. Again I ascended the hill. The whole country was now bathed in a rejoicing sunlight. The warm verdure was bursting all round me. Teams were a-field. Birds, newly arrived from the South, were blithely singing in the air. Even the crows cawed with a certain unction, and seemed a shade or two less black than usual.

Hark! there goes the cock! How shall I describe the crow of the Shanghai at noontide! His sunrise crow was a whisper to it. It was the loudest, longest and most strangely musical crow that ever amazed mortal man. I had heard plenty of cock-crows before, and many fine ones;—but this one! so smooth, and flutelike in its very clamor—so self-possessed in its very rapture of exultation—so vast, mounting, swelling, soaring, as if spurted out from a golden throat, thrown far back. Nor did it sound like the foolish, vain-glorious crow of some young sophomorean cock, who knew not the world, and was beginning life in audacious gay spirits, because in wretched ignorance of what might be to come. It was the crow of a cock who crowed not without advice; the crow of a cock who knew a thing or two; the crow of a cock who had fought the world and got the better of it and was resolved to crow, though the earth should heave and the heavens should fall. It was a wise crow; an invincible crow; a philosophic crow; a crow of all crows.

I returned home once more full of reinvigorated spirits, with a dauntless sort of feeling. I thought over my debts and other troubles, and over the unlucky risings of the poor oppressed peoples abroad, and over the railroad and steamboat accidents, and over even the loss of my dear friend, with a calm, good-natured rapture of defiance, which astounded myself. I felt as though I could meet Death, and invite him to dinner, and toast the Catacombs with him, in pure overflow of self-reliance and a sense of universal security.

Toward evening I went up to the hill once more to find whether, indeed, the glorious cock would prove game even from the rising of the sun unto the going down thereof. Talk of Vespers or Curfew!—the evening crow of the cock went out of his mighty throat all over the land and inhabited it, like Xerxes from the East with his double-winged host. It was miraculous. Bless me, what a crow! The cock went game to roost that night, depend upon it, victorious over the entire day, and bequeathing the echoes of his thousand crows to night.

After an unwontedly sound, refreshing sleep I rose early, feeling like a carriage-spring—light—elliptical—airy—buoyant as sturgeon-nose—and, like a foot-ball, bounded up the hill. Hark! Shanghai was up before me. The early bird that caught the worm—crowing like a bugle worked by an engine—lusty, loud, all jubilation. From the scattered farmhouses a multitude of other cocks were crowing, and replying to each other's crows. But they were as flageolets to a trombone. Shanghai would suddenly break in, and overwhelm all their crows with his one domineering blast. He seemed to have nothing to do with any other concern. He replied to no other crow, but crowed solely by himself, on his own account, in solitary scorn and independence.

Oh, brave cock!—oh, noble Shanghai!—oh, bird rightly offered up by the invincible Socrates, in testimony of his final victory over life.

As I live, thought I, this blessed day, will I go and seek out the Shanghai, and buy him, if I have to clap another mortgage on my land.

I listened attentively now, striving to mark from what direction the crow came. But it so charged and replenished, and made bountiful and overflowing all the air, that it was impossible to say from what precise point the exultation came. All that I could decide upon was this: the crow came from out of the east, and not from out of the west. I then considered with myself how far a cock-crow might be heard. In this still country, shut in, too, by mountains, sounds were audible at great distances. Besides, the undulations of the land, the abuttings of the mountains into the rolling hill and valley below, produced strange echoes, and reverberations, and multiplications, and accumulations of resonance, very remarkable to hear, and very puzzling to think of. Where lurked this valiant Shanghai—this bird of cheerful Socrates—the game-fowl Greek who died unappalled? Where lurked he? Oh, noble cock, where are you? Crow once more, my Bantam! my princely, my imperial Shanghai! my bird of the Emperor of China! Brother of the sun! Cousin of great Jove! where are you?—one crow more, and tell me your number!

Hark! like a full orchestra of the cocks of all nations, forth burst the crow. But where from? There it is; but where? There was no telling, further than it came from out of the east.

After breakfast I took my stick and sallied down the road. There were many gentlemen's seats dotting the neighboring country, and I made no doubt that some of these opulent gentlemen had invested a hundred dollar bill in some royal Shanghai recently imported in the ship Trade Wind, or the ship White Squall, or the ship Sovereign of the Seas; for it must needs have been a brave ship with a brave name which bore the fortunes of so brave a cock. I resolved to walk the entire country, and find this noble foreigner out; but thought it would not be amiss to inquire on the way at the humblest homesteads, whether, peradventure, they had heard of a lately-imported Shanghai belonging to any gentlemen settlers from the city; for it was plain that no poor farmer, no poor man of any sort, could own such an Oriental trophy—such a Great Bell of St. Paul's swung in a cock's throat.

I met an old man, plowing, in a field nigh the road-side fence.

"My friend, have you heard an extraordinary cock-crow of late?"

"Well, well," he drawled, "I don't know—the Widow Crowfoot has a cock—and Squire Squaretoes has a cock—and I have a cock, and they all crow. But I don't know of any on 'em with 'straordinary crows."

"Good-morning to you," said I, shortly; "it's plain that you have not heard the crow of the Emperor of China's chanticleer."

Presently I met another old man mending a tumble-down old rail-fence. The rails were rotten, and at every move of the old man's hand they crumbled into yellow ochre. He had much better let the fence alone, or else get him new rails. And here I must say, that one cause of the sad fact why idiocy more prevails among farmers than any other class of people, is owing to their undertaking the mending of rotten rail-fences in warm, relaxing spring weather. The enterprise is a hopeless one. It is a laborious one; it is a bootless one. It is an enterprise to make the heart break. Vast pains squandered upon a vanity. For how can one make rotten rail-fences stand up on their rotten pins? By what magic put pitch into sticks which have lain freezing and baking through sixty consecutive winters and summers? This it is, this wretched endeavor to mend rotten rail-fences with their own rotten rails, which drives many farmers into the asylum.

On the face of the old man in question incipient idiocy was plainly marked. For, about sixty rods before him extended one of the most unhappy and desponding broken-hearted Virginia rail-fences I ever saw in my life. While in a field behind, were a set of young steers, possessed as by devils, continually butting at this forlorn old fence, and breaking through it here and there, causing the old man to drop his work and chase them back within bounds. He would chase them with a piece of rail huge as Goliath's beam, but as light as cork. At the first flourish, it crumbled into powder.

"My friend," said I, addressing this woeful mortal, "have you heard an extraordinary cock-crow of late?"

I might as well as have asked him if he had heard the death-tick. He stared at me with a long, bewildered, doleful, and unutterable stare, and without reply resumed his unhappy labors.

What a fool, thought I, to have asked such an uncheerful and uncheerable creature about a cheerful cock!

I walked on. I had now descended the high land where my house stood, and being in a low tract could not hear the crow of the Shanghai, which doubtless overshot me there. Besides, the Shanghai might be at lunch of corn and oats, or taking a nap, and so interrupted his jubilations for a while.

At length, I encountered riding along the road, a portly gentleman—nay, a *pursy* one—of great wealth, who had recently purchased him some noble acres, and built him a noble mansion, with a goodly fowl-house attached, the fame whereof spread through all the country. Thought I, Here now is the owner of the Shanghai.

"Sir," said I, "excuse me, but I am a countryman of yours, and would ask, if so be you own any Shanghais?"

"Oh, yes; I have ten Shanghais."

"Ten!" exclaimed I, in wonder; "and do they all crow?"

"Most lustily; every soul of them; I wouldn't own a cock that wouldn't crow."

"Will you turn back, and show me those Shanghais?"

"With pleasure: I am proud of them. They cost me, in the lump, six hundred dollars."

As I walked by the side of his horse, I was thinking to myself whether possibly I had not mistaken the harmoniously combined crowings of ten Shanghais in a squad, for the supernatural crow of a single Shanghai by himself.

"Sir," said I, "is there one of your Shanghais which far exceeds all the others in the lustiness, musicalness, and inspiring effects of his crow?"

"They crow pretty much alike, I believe," he courteously replied. "I really don't know that I could tell their crow apart."

I began to think that after all my noble chanticleer might not be in the possession of this wealthy gentleman. However, we went into his fowl-yard, and saw his Shanghais. Let me say that hitherto I had never clapped eye on this species of imported fowl. I had heard what enormous prices were paid for them, and also that they were of an enormous size, and had somehow fancied they must be of a beauty and brilliancy proportioned both to size and price. What was my surprise, then, to see ten carrot-colored monsters, without the smallest pretension to effulgence of plumage. Immediately, I determined that my royal cock was neither among these, nor could possibly be a Shanghai at all; if these gigantic gallows-bird fowl were fair specimens of the true Shanghai.

I walked all day, dining and resting at a farmhouse, inspecting various fowl-yards, interrogating various owners of fowls, hearkening to various crows, but discovered not the mysterious chanticleer. Indeed, I had wandered so far and deviously, that I could not hear his crow. I began to suspect that this cock was a mere visitor in the country, who had taken his departure by the eleven o'clock train for the South, and was now crowing and jubilating somewhere on the verdant banks of Long Island Sound.

But next morning, again I heard the inspiring blast, again felt my blood bound in me, again felt superior to all the ills of life, again felt like turning my dun out of doors. But displeased with the reception given him at his last visit, the dun stayed away, doubtless being in a huff. Silly fellow that he was to take a harmless joke in earnest.

Several days passed, during which I made sundry excursions in the regions roundabout, but in vain sought the cock. Still, I heard him from the hill, and sometimes from the house, and sometimes in the stillness of the night. If at times I would relapse into my doleful dumps straightway at the sound of the exultant and defiant crow, my soul, too, would turn chanticleer, and clap her wings, and throw back her throat, and breathe forth a cheerful challenge to all the world of woes.

At last, after some weeks I was necessitated to clap another mortgage on my estate, in order to pay certain debts, and among others the one I owed the dun, who of late had commenced a civil-process against me. The way the process was served was a most insulting one. In a private room I had been enjoying myself in the village tavern over a bottle of Philadelphia porter, and some Herkimer cheese, and a roll, and having apprised the landlord, who was a friend of mine, that I would settle with him when I received my next remittances, stepped to the peg where I had hung my hat in the bar-room, to get a choice cigar I had left in the hall, when lo! I found the civil-process enveloping the cigar. When I unrolled the cigar, I unrolled the civil-process, and the constable standing by rolled out, with a thick tongue, "Take notice!" and added, in a whisper, "Put that in your pipe and smoke it!"

I turned short round upon the gentlemen then and there present in that bar-room. Said I, "Gentlemen, is this an honorable—nay, is this a lawful way of serving a civil-process? Behold!"

One and all they were of opinion, that it was a highly inelegant act in the constable to take advantage of a gentleman's lunching on cheese and porter, to be so uncivil as to slip a civil-process into his hat. It was ungenerous; it was cruel; for the sudden shock of the thing coming instanter upon the lunch, would impair the proper digestion of the cheese, which is proverbially not so easy of digestion as *blanc-mange*.

Arrived at home I read the process, and felt a twinge of melancholy. Hard world! hard world! Here I am, as good a fellow as ever lived— hospitable—open-hearted—generous to a fault; and the Fates forbid that I should possess the fortune to bless the country with my bounteousness. Nay, while many a stingy curmudgeon rolls in idle gold, I, heart of nobleness as I am, I have civil-processes served on me! I bowed my head, and felt forlorn—unjustly used—abused—unappreciated—in short, miserable.

Hark! like a clarion! yea, like a bolt of thunder with bells to it—came the all-glorious and defiant crow! Ye gods, how it set me up again! Right on my pins! Yes, verily on stilts!

Oh, noble cock!

Plain as cock could speak, it said, "Let the world and all aboard of it go to pot. Do you be jolly, and never say die! What's the world compared to you? What is it, anyhow, but a lump of loam? Do you be jolly!"

Oh, noble cock!

"But my dear and glorious cock," mused I, upon second thought, "one can't so easily send this world to pot; one can't so easily be jolly with civil-processes in his hat or hand."

Hark! the crow again. Plain as cock could speak, it said: "Hang the process, and hang the fellow that sent it! If you have not land or cash, go and thrash the fellow, and tell him you never mean to pay him. Be jolly!"

Now this was the way—through the imperative intimations of the cock—that I came to clap the added mortgage on my estate; paid all my debts by fusing them into this one added bond and mortgage. Thus made at ease again, I renewed my search for the noble cock. But in vain, though I heard him every day. I began to think there was some sort of deception in this mysterious thing: some wonderful ventriloquist prowled around my barns, or in my cellar, or on my roof, and was minded to be gayly mischievous. But no—what ventriloquist could so crow with such an heroic and celestial crow?

At last, one morning there came to me a certain singular man, who had sawed and split my wood in March—some five-and-thirty cords of it—and now he came for his pay. He was a singular man, I say. He was tall and spare, with a long saddish face, yet somehow a latently joyous eye, which offered the strangest contrast. His air seemed staid, but undepressed. He wore a long, gray, shabby coat, and a big battered hat. This man had sawed my wood at so much a cord. He would stand and saw all day in a driving snow-storm, and never wink at it. He never spoke unless spoken to. He only sawed. Saw, saw, saw—snow, snow, snow. The saw and the snow went together like two natural things. The first day this man came, he brought his dinner with him, and volunteered to eat it sitting on his buck in the snow-storm. From my window, where I was reading Burton's *Anatomy of Melancholy*, I saw him in the act. I burst out of doors bareheaded. "Good heavens!" cried I; "what are you doing? Come in. *This* your dinner!"

He had a hunk of stale bread and another hunk of salt beef, wrapped in a wet newspaper, and washed his morsels down by melting a handful of fresh snow in his mouth. I took this rash man indoors, planted him by the fire, gave him a dish of hot pork and beans, and a mug of cider.

"Now," said I, "don't you bring any of your damp dinners here. You work by the job, to be sure; but I'll dine you for all that."

He expressed his acknowledgments in a calm, proud, but not ungrateful way, and dispatched his meal with satisfaction to himself, and me also. It afforded me pleasure to perceive that he quaffed down his mug of cider like a man. I honored him. When I addressed him in the way of business at his buck, I did so in a guardedly respectful and deferential manner. Interested in his singular aspect, struck by his wondrous intensity of application at his saw—a most wearisome and disgustful occupation to most people—I often sought to gather from him who he was, what sort of a life he led, where he was born, and so on. But he was mum. He came to saw my wood, and eat my dinners—if I chose to offer them—but not to gabble. At first, I somewhat resented his sullen silence under the circumstances. But better considering it, I honored him the more. I increased the respectfulness and deferentialness of my address toward him. I concluded within myself that this man had experienced hard times; that he had had many sore rubs in the world; that he was of a solemn disposition; that he was of the mind of Solomon; that he lived calmly, decorously, temperately; and though a very poor man, was, nevertheless, a highly respectable one. At times I imagined that he might even be an elder or deacon of some small country church. I thought it would not be a bad plan to run this excellent man for President of the United States. He would prove a great reformer of abuses.

His name was Merrymusk. I had often thought how jolly a name for so unjolly a wight. I inquired of people whether they knew Merrymusk. But it was some time before I learned much about him. He was by birth a Marylander, it appeared, who had long lived in the country round about; a wandering man; until within some ten years ago, a thriftless man, though perfectly innocent of crime; a man who would work hard a month with surprising soberness, and then spend all his wages in one riotous night. In youth he had been a sailor, and run away from his ship at Batavia, where he caught the fever, and came nigh dying. But he rallied, reshipped, landed home, found all his friends dead, and struck for the Northern interior, where he had since tarried. Nine years back he had married a wife, and now had four children. His wife was become a perfect invalid; one child had the white-swelling and the rest were rickety. He and his family lived in a shanty on a lonely barren patch nigh the railroad track, where it passed close to the base of the mountain. He had bought a fine cow to have plenty of wholesome milk for his children; but the cow died during an accouchement, and he could not afford to buy another. Still, his family never suffered for lack of food. He worked hard and brought it to them.

Now, as I said before, having long previously sawed my wood, this Merrymusk came for his pay.

"My friend," said I, "do you know of any gentleman hereabouts who owns an extraordinary cock?"

The twinkle glittered quite plain in the wood-sawyer's eye.

"I know of no *gentleman*," he replied, "who has what might well be called an extraordinary cock."

Oh, thought I, this Merrymusk is not the man to enlighten me. I am afraid I shall never discover this extraordinary cock.

Not having the full change to pay Merrymusk, I gave him his due, as nigh as I could make it, and told him that in a day or two I would take a walk and visit his place, and hand to him the remainder. Accordingly one fine morning I sallied forth upon the errand. I had much ado finding the best road to the shanty. No one seemed to know where it was exactly. It lay in a very lonely part of the country, a densely-wooded mountain on one side (which I call October Mountain, on account of its bannered aspect in that month), and a thicketed swamp on the other, the railroad cutting the swamp. Straight as a die the railroad cut it; many times a day tantalizing the wretched shanty with the sight of all the beauty, rank, fashion, health, trunks, silver and gold, dry-goods and groceries, brides and grooms, happy wives and husbands, flying by the lonely door—no time to stop—flash! here they are—and there they go! out of sight at both ends—as if that part of the world were only made to fly over, and not to settle upon. And this was about all the shanty saw of what people call life.

Though puzzled somewhat, yet I knew the general direction where the shanty lay, and on I trudged. As I advanced, I was surprised to hear the mysterious cock crow with more and more distinctness. Is it possible, thought I, that any gentleman owning a Shanghai can dwell in such a lonesome, dreary region? Louder and louder, nigher and nigher, sounded the glorious and defiant clarion. Though somehow I may be out of the track to my wood-sawyer's, I said to myself, yet, thank heaven, I seem to be on the way toward that extraordinary cock. I was delighted with this auspicious accident. On I journeyed; while at intervals the crow sounded most invitingly, and jocundly, and superbly; and the last crow was ever nigher than the former one. At last, emerging from a thicket of elders, straight before me I saw the most resplendent creature that ever blessed the sight of man.

A cock, more like a golden eagle than a cock. A cock, more like a field marshal than a cock. A cock, more like Lord Nelson with all his glittering arms on, standing on the Vanguard's quarter-deck going into battle, than a cock. A cock, more like the Emperor Charlemagne in his robes at Aix la Chapelle, than a cock.

Such a cock!

He was of a haughty size, stood haughtily on his haughty legs. His colors were red, gold, and white. The red was on his crest along, which was a mighty and symmetric crest, like unto Hector's helmet, as delineated on antique shields. His plumage was snowy, traced with gold. He walked in front of the shanty, like a peer of the realm; his crest lifted, his chest heaved out, his embroidered trappings flashing in the light. His pace was wonderful. He looked like some Oriental king in some magnificent Italian opera.

Merrymusk advanced from the door.

"Pray is not that the Signor Beneventano?"

"Sir!"

"That's the cock," said I, a little embarrassed. The truth was, my enthusiasm had betrayed me into a rather silly inadvertence. I had made a somewhat learned sort of allusion in the presence of an unlearned man. Consequently, upon discovering it by his honest stare, I felt foolish; but carried it off by declaring that *this was the cock.*

Now, during the preceding autumn I had been to the city, and had chanced to be present at a performance of the Italian Opera. In that opera figured in some royal character a certain Signor Beneventano—a man of a tall, imposing person, clad in rich raiment, like to plumage, and with a most remarkable, majestic, scornful stride. The Signor Beneventano seemed on the point of tumbling over backward with exceeding haughtiness. And, for all the world, the proud pace of the cock seemed the very stage-pace of the Signor Beneventano.

Hark! suddenly the cock paused, lifted his head still higher, ruffled his plumes, seemed inspired, and sent forth a lusty crow. October Mountain echoed it; other mountains sent it back; still others rebounded it; it overran the country round. Now I plainly perceived how it was I had chanced to hear the gladdening sound on my distant hill.

"Good heavens! do you own the cock? Is that cock yours?"

"Is it my cock!" said Merrymusk, looking slyly gleeful out of the corner of his long, solemn face.

"Where did you get it?"

"It chipped the shell here. I raised it."

"You?"

Hark? Another crow. It might have raised the ghosts of all the pines and hemlocks ever cut down in that country. Marvelous cock! Having crowed, he strode on again, surrounded by a bevy of admiring hens.

"What will you take for Signor Beneventano?"

"Sir?"

"That magic cock—what will you take for him?"

"I won't sell him."

"I will give you fifty dollars."

"Pooh!"

"One hundred!"

"Pish!"

"Five hundred!"

"Bah!"

"And you a poor man."

"No; don't I own that cock, and haven't I refused five hundred dollars for him?"

"True," said I, in profound thought; "that's a fact. You won't sell him, then?"

"No."

"Will you give him?"

"No."

"Will you *keep* him, then!" I shouted, in a rage.

"Yes."

I stood awhile admiring the cock, and wondering at the man. At last I felt a redoubled admiration of the one, and a redoubled deference for the other.

"Won't you step in?" said Merrymusk.

"But won't the cock be prevailed upon to join us?" said I.

"Yes. Trumpet! hither, boy! hither!"

The cock turned round, and strode up to Merrymusk.

"Come!"

The cock followed us into the shanty.

"Crow!"

The roof jarred.

Oh, noble cock!

I turned in silence upon my entertainer. There he sat on an old battered chest, in his old battered gray coat, with patches at his knees and elbows, and a deplorably bunged hat. I glanced round the room. Bare rafters overhead, but solid junks of jerked beef hanging from them. Earth floor, but a heap of potatoes in one corner, and a sack of Indian meal in another. A blanket was strung across the apartment at the further end, from which came a woman's ailing voice and the voices of ailing children. But somehow in the ailing of these voices there seemed no complaint.

"Mrs. Merrymusk and children?"

"Yes."

I looked at the cock. There he stood majestically in the middle of the room. He looked like a Spanish grandee caught in a shower, and standing under some peasant's shed. There was a strange supernatural look of contrast about him. He irradiated the shanty; he glorified its meanness. He glorified the battered chest, and tattered gray coat, and the bunged hat. He glorified the very voices which came in ailing tones from behind the screen.

"Oh, father," cried a little sickly voice, "let Trumpet sound again."

"Crow," cried Merrymusk.

The cock threw himself into a posture. The roof jarred.

"Does not this disturb Mrs. Merrymusk and the sick children?"

"Crow again, Trumpet."

The roof jarred.

"It does not disturb them, then?"

"Didn't you hear 'em *ask* for it?"

"How is it, that your sick family like this crowing?" said I. "The cock is a glorious cock, with a glorious voice, but not exactly the sort of thing for a sick chamber, one would suppose. Do they really like it?"

"Don't *you* like it? Don't it do *you* good? Ain't it inspiring? Don't it impart pluck? give stuff against despair?"

"All true," said I, removing my hat with profound humility before the brave spirit disguised in the base coat.

"But then," said I, still with some misgivings, "so loud, so wonderfully clamorous a crow, methinks might be amiss to invalids, and retard their convalescence."

"Crow your best now, Trumpet!"

I leaped from my chair. The cock frightened me, like some overpowering angel in the Apocalypse. He seemed crowing over the fall of wicked Babylon, or crowing over the triumph of righteous Joshua in the vale of Askelon. When I regained my composure somewhat, an inquisitive thought occurred to me. I resolved to gratify it.

"Merrymusk, will you present me to your wife and children?"

"Yes. Wife, the gentleman wants to step in."

"He is very welcome," replied a weak voice.

Going behind the curtain, there lay a wasted, but strangely cheerful human face; and that was pretty much all; the body, hid by the counterpane and an old coat, seemed too shrunken to reveal itself through such impediments. At the bedside sat a pale girl, ministering. In another bed lay three children, side by side; three more pale faces.

"Oh, father, we don't mislike the gentleman, but let us see Trumpet too."

At a word, the cock strode behind the screen, and perched himself on the children's bed. All their wasted eyes gazed at him with a wild and spiritual delight. They seemed to sun themselves in the radiant plumage of the cock.

"Better than a 'pothecary, eh," said Merrymusk. "This is Dr. Cock himself."

We retired from the sick ones, and I reseated myself again, lost in thought, over this strange household.

"You seem a glorious independent fellow," said I.

"And I don't think you a fool, and never did. Sir, you are a trump."

"Is there any hope of your wife's recovery?" said I, modestly seeking to turn the conversation.

"Not the least."

"The children?"

"Very little."

"It must be a doleful life, then, for all concerned. This lonely solitude—this shanty—hard work—hard times."

"Haven't I Trumpet? He's the cheerer. He crows through all; crows at the darkest: Glory to God in the highest! Continually he crows it."

"Just the import I first ascribed to his crow, Merrymusk, when first I heard it from my hill. I thought some rich nabob owned some costly Shanghai; little weening any such poor man as you owned this lusty cock of a domestic breed."

"*Poor* man like *me*? Why call *me* poor? Don't the cock *I* own glorify this otherwise inglorious, lean, lantern-jawed land? Didn't *my* cock encourage *you*? And *I* give you all this glorification away gratis. I am a great philanthropist. I am a rich man—a very rich man, and a very happy one. Crow, Trumpet."

The roof jarred.

I returned home in a deep mood. I was not wholly at rest concerning the soundness of Merrymusk's views of things, though full of admiration for him. I was thinking on the matter before my door, when I heard the cock crow again. Enough. Merrymusk is right.

Oh, noble cock! oh, noble man!

I did not see Merrymusk for some weeks after this; but hearing the glorious and rejoicing crow, I supposed that all went as usual with him. My own frame of mind remained a rejoicing one. The cock still inspired me. I saw another mortgage piled on my plantation; but only bought another dozen of stout, and a dozen-dozen of Philadelphia porter. Some of my relatives died; I wore no mourning, but for three days drank stout in preference to porter, stout being of the darker color. I heard the cock crow the instant I received the unwelcome tidings.

"Your health in this stout, oh, noble cock!"

I thought I would call on Merrymusk again, not having seen or heard of him for some time now. Approaching the place, there were no signs of motion about the shanty. I felt a strange misgiving. But the cock crew from within doors, and the boding vanished. I knocked at the door. A feeble voice bade me enter. The curtain was no longer drawn; the whole house was a hospital now. Merrymusk lay on a heap of old clothes; wife and children were all in their beds. The cock was perched on an old hogshead hoop, swung from the ridge-pole in the middle of the shanty.

"You are sick, Merrymusk," said I mournfully.

"No, I am well," he feebly answered.—

"Crow, Trumpet."

I shrunk. The strong soul in the feeble body appalled me.

But the cock crew.

The roof jarred.

"How is Mrs. Merrymusk?"

"Well."

"And the children?"

"Well. All well."

The last two words he shouted forth in a kind of wild ecstasy of triumph over ill. It was too much. His head fell back. A white napkin seemed dropped upon his face. Merrymusk was dead.

An awful fear seized me.

But the cock crew.

The cock shook his plumage as if each feather were a banner. The cock hung from the shanty roof as erewhile the trophied flags from the dome of St. Paul's. The cock terrified me with exceeding wonder.

I drew nigh the bedsides of the woman and children. They marked my look of strange affright; they knew what had happened.

"My good man is just dead," breathed the woman lowly. "Tell me true?"

"Dead," said I.

The cock crew.

She fell back, without a sigh, and through long-loving sympathy was dead.

The cock crew.

The cock shook sparkles from his golden plumage. The cock seemed in a rapture of benevolent delight. Leaping from the hoop, he strode up majestically to the pile of old clothes, where the wood-sawyer lay, and planted himself, like an armorial supporter, at his side. Then raised one long, musical, triumphant, and final sort of a crow, with throat heaved far back, as if he meant the blast to waft the wood-sawyer's soul sheer up to the seventh heavens. Then he strode, king-like, to the woman's bed. Another upturned and exultant crow, mated to the former.

The pallor of the children was changed to radiance. Their faces shone celestially through grime and dirt. They seemed children of emperors and kings, disguised. The cock sprang upon their bed, shook himself, and crowed, and crowed again, and still and still again. He seemed bent upon crowing the souls of the children out of their wasted bodies. He seemed bent upon rejoining instanter this whole family in the upper air. The children seemed to second his endeavors. Far, deep, intense longings for release transfigured them into spirits before my eyes. I saw angels where they lay.

They were dead.

The cock shook his plumage over them. The cock crew. It was now like a Bravo! like a Hurrah! like a Three-times-three! hip! hip! He strode out of the shanty. I followed. He flew upon the apex of the dwelling, spread wide his wings, sounded one supernatural note, and dropped at my feet.

The cock was dead.

If now you visit that hilly region, you will see, nigh the railroad track, just beneath October Mountain, on the other side of the swamp—there you will see a gravestone, not with skull and cross-bones, but with a lusty cock in act of crowing, chiseled on it, with the words beneath:

"*O death, where is thy sting? O grave, where is thy victory?*"

The wood-sawyer and his family, with the Signor Beneventano, lie in that spot; and I buried them, and planted the stone, which was a stone made to order; and never since then have I felt the doleful dumps, but under all circumstances crow late and early with a continual crow.

Cock-a-Doodle-Doo!—oo!—oo!—oo!—oo!

THE FIDDLER

So my poem is damned, and immortal fame is not for me! I am nobody forever and ever. Intolerable fate!

Snatching my hat, I dashed down the criticism and rushed out into Broadway, where enthusiastic throngs were crowding to a circus in a side-street near by, very recently started, and famous for a capital clown.

Presently my old friend Standard rather boisterously accosted me.

"Well met, Helmstone, my boy! Ah! what's the matter? Haven't been committing murder? Ain't flying justice? You look wild!"

"You have seen it, then!" said I, of course referring to the criticism.

"Oh, yes; I was there at the morning performance. Great clown, I assure you. But here comes Hautboy. Hautboy—Helmstone."

Without having time or inclination to resent so mortifying a mistake, I was instantly soothed as I gazed on the face of the new acquaintance so unceremoniously introduced. His person was short and full, with a juvenile, animated cast to it. His complexion rurally ruddy; his eye sincere, cheery, and gray. His hair alone betrayed that he was not an overgrown boy. From his hair I set him down as forty or more.

"Come, Standard," he gleefully cried to my friend, "are you not going to the circus? The clown is inimitable, they say. Come, Mr. Helmstone, too—come both; and circus over, we'll take a nice stew and punch at Taylor's."

The sterling content, good-humor, and extraordinary ruddy, sincere expression of this most singular new acquaintance acted upon me like magic. It seemed mere loyalty to human nature to accept an invitation from so unmistakably kind and honest a heart.

During the circus performance I kept my eye more on Hautboy than on the celebrated clown. Hautboy was the sight for me. Such genuine enjoyment as his struck me to the soul with a sense of the reality of the thing called happiness. The jokes of the clown he seemed to roll under his tongue as ripe magnumbonums. Now the foot, now the hand, was employed to attest his grateful applause. At any hit more than ordinary, he turned upon Standard and me to see if his rare pleasure was shared. In a man of forty I saw a boy of twelve; and this too without the slightest abatement of my respect. Because all was so honest and natural, every expression and attitude so graceful with genuine good-nature, that the marvelous juvenility of Hautboy assumed a sort of divine and immortal air, like that of some forever youthful god of Greece.

But much as I gazed upon Hautboy, and much as I admired his air, yet that desperate mood in which I had first rushed from the house had not so entirely departed as not to molest me with momentary returns. But from these relapses I would rouse myself, and swiftly glance round the broad amphitheatre of eagerly interested and all-applauding human faces. Hark! claps, thumps, deafening huzzas; the vast assembly seemed frantic with acclamation; and what, mused I, has caused all this? Why, the clown only comically grinned with one of his extra grins.

Then I repeated in my mind that sublime passage in my poem, in which Cleothemes the Argive vindicates the justice of the war. Ay, ay, thought I to myself, did I now leap into the ring there, and repeat that identical passage, nay, enact the whole tragic poem before them, would they applaud the poet as they applaud the clown? No! They would hoot me, and call me doting or mad. Then what does this prove? Your infatuation or their insensibility? Perhaps both; but indubitably the first. But why wail? Do you seek admiration from the admirers of a buffoon? Call to mind the saying of the Athenian, who, when the people vociferously applauded in the forum, asked his friend in a whisper, what foolish thing had he said?

Again my eye swept the circus, and fell on the ruddy radiance of the countenance of Hautboy. But its clear honest cheeriness disdained my disdain. My intolerant pride was rebuked. And yet Hautboy dreamed not what magic reproof to a soul like mine sat on his laughing brow. At the very instant I felt the dart of the censure, his eye twinkled, his hand waved, his voice was lifted in jubilant delight at another joke of the inexhaustible clown.

Circus over, we went to Taylor's. Among crowds of others, we sat down to our stews and punches at one of the small marble tables. Hautboy sat opposite to me. Though greatly subdued from its former hilarity, his face still shone with gladness. But added to this was a quality not so prominent before; a certain serene expression of leisurely, deep good sense. Good sense and good humor in him joined hands. As the conversation proceeded between the brisk Standard and him—for I said little or nothing—I was more and more struck with the excellent judgment he evinced. In most of his remarks upon a variety of topics Hautboy seemed intuitively to hit the exact line between enthusiasm and apathy. It was plain that while Hautboy saw the world pretty much as it was, yet he did not theoretically espouse its bright side nor its dark side. Rejecting all solutions, he but acknowledged facts. What was sad in the world he did not superficially gainsay; what was glad in it he did not cynically slur; and all which was to him personally enjoyable, he gratefully took to his heart. It was plain, then—so it seemed at that moment, at least—that his extraordinary cheerfulness did not arise either from deficiency of feeling or thought.

Suddenly remembering an engagement, he took up his hat, bowed pleasantly, and left us.

"Well, Helmstone," said Standard, inaudibly drumming on the slab, "what do you think of your new acquaintance?"

The last two words tingled with a peculiar and novel significance.

"New acquaintance indeed," echoed I. "Standard, I owe you a thousand thanks for introducing me to one of the most singular men I have ever seen. It needed the optical sight of such a man to believe in the possibility of his existence."

"You rather like him, then," said Standard, with ironical dryness.

"I hugely love and admire him, Standard. I wish I were Hautboy."

"Ah? That's a pity now. There's only one Hautboy in the world."

This last remark set me to pondering again, and somehow it revived my dark mood.

"His wonderful cheerfulness, I suppose," said I, sneering with spleen, "originates not less in a felicitous fortune than in a felicitous temper. His great good sense is apparent; but great good sense may exist without sublime endowments. Nay, I take it, in certain cases, that good sense is simply owing to the absence of those. Much more, cheerfulness. Unpossessed of genius, Hautboy is eternally blessed."

"Ah? You would not think him an extraordinary genius then?"

"Genius? What! Such a short, fat fellow a genius! Genius, like Cassius, is lank."

"Ah? But could you not fancy that Hautboy might formerly have had genius, but luckily getting rid of it, at last fatted up?"

"For a genius to get rid of his genius is as impossible as for a man in the galloping consumption to get rid of that."

"Ah? You speak very decidedly."

"Yes, Standard," cried I, increasing in spleen, "your cheery Hautboy, after all, is no pattern, no lesson for you and me. With average abilities; opinions clear, because circumscribed; passions docile, because they are feeble; a temper hilarious, because he was born to it—how can your Hautboy be made a reasonable example to a heady fellow like you, or an ambitious dreamer like me? Nothing tempts him beyond common limit; in himself he has nothing to restrain. By constitution he is exempted from all moral harm. Could ambition but prick him; had he but once heard applause, or endured contempt, a very different man would your Hautboy be. Acquiescent and calm from the cradle to the grave, he obviously slides through the crowd."

"Ah?"

"Why do you say *ah* to me so strangely whenever I speak?"

"Did you ever hear of Master Betty?"

"The great English prodigy, who long ago ousted the Siddons and the Kembles from Drury Lane, and made the whole town run mad with acclamation?"

"The same," said Standard, once more inaudibly drumming on the slab.

I looked at him perplexed. He seemed to be holding the master-key of our theme in mysterious reserve; seemed to be throwing out his Master Betty too, to puzzle me only the more.

"What under heaven can Master Betty, the great genius and prodigy, an English boy twelve years old, have to do with the poor commonplace plodder Hautboy, an American of forty?"

"Oh, nothing in the least. I don't imagine that they ever saw each other. Besides, Master Betty must be dead and buried long ere this."

"Then why cross the ocean, and rifle the grave to drag his remains into this living discussion?"

"Absent-mindedness, I suppose. I humbly beg pardon. Proceed with your observations on Hautboy. You think he never had genius, quite too contented and happy, and fat for that—ah? You think him no pattern for men in general? affording no lesson of value to neglected merit, genius ignored, or impotent presumption rebuked?—all of which three amount to much the same thing. You admire his cheerfulness, while scorning his commonplace soul. Poor Hautboy, how sad that your very cheerfulness should, by a by-blow, bring you despite!"

"I don't say I scorn him; you are unjust. I simply declare that he is no pattern for me."

A sudden noise at my side attracted my ear. Turning, I saw Hautboy again, who very blithely reseated himself on the chair he had left.

"I was behind time with my engagement," said Hautboy, "so thought I would run back and rejoin you. But come, you have sat long enough here. Let us go to my rooms. It is only five minutes' walk."

"If you will promise to fiddle for us, we will," said Standard.

Fiddle! thought I—he's a jigembob *fiddler* then? No wonder genius declines to measure its pace to a fiddler's bow. My spleen was very strong on me now.

"I will gladly fiddle you your fill," replied Hautboy to Standard. "Come on."

In a few minutes we found ourselves in the fifth story of a sort of storehouse, in a lateral street to Broadway. It was curiously furnished with all sorts of odd furniture which seemed to have been obtained, piece by piece, at auctions of old-fashioned household stuff. But all was charmingly clean and cosy.

Pressed by Standard, Hautboy forthwith got out his dented old fiddle, and sitting down on a tall rickety stool, played away right merrily at Yankee Doodle and other off-handed, dashing, and disdainfully care-free airs. But common as were the tunes, I was transfixed by something miraculously superior in the style. Sitting there on the old stool, his rusty hat sideways cocked on his head, one foot dangling adrift, he plied the bow of an enchanter. All my moody discontent, every vestige of peevishness fled. My whole splenetic soul capitulated to the magical fiddle.

"Something of an Orpheus, ah?" said Standard, archly nudging me beneath the left rib.

"And I, the charmed Bruin," murmured I.

The fiddle ceased. Once more, with redoubled curiosity, I gazed upon the easy, indifferent Hautboy. But he entirely baffled inquisition.

When, leaving him, Standard and I were in the street once more, I earnestly conjured him to tell me who, in sober truth, this marvelous Hautboy was.

"Why, haven't you seen him? And didn't you yourself lay his whole anatomy open on the marble slab at Taylor's? What more can you possibly learn? Doubtless your own masterly insight has already put you in possession of all."

"You mock me, Standard. There is some mystery here. Tell me, I entreat you, who is Hautboy?"

"An extraordinary genius, Helmstone," said Standard, with sudden ardor, "who in boyhood drained the whole flagon of glory; whose going from city to city was a going from triumph to triumph. One who has been an object of wonder to the wisest, been caressed by the loveliest, received the open homage of thousands on thousands of the rabble. But to-day he walks Broadway and no man knows him. With you and me, the elbow of the hurrying clerk, and the pole of the remorseless omnibus, shove him. He who has a hundred times been crowned with laurels, now wears, as you see, a bunged beaver. Once fortune poured showers of gold into his lap, as showers of laurel leaves upon his brow. To-day, from house to house he hies, teaching fiddling for a living. Crammed once with fame, he is now hilarious without it. *With* genius and *without* fame, he is happier than a king. More a prodigy now than ever."

"His true name?"

"Let me whisper it in your ear."

"What! Oh, Standard, myself, as a child, have shouted myself hoarse applauding that very name in the theatre."

"I have heard your poem was not very handsomely received," said Standard, now suddenly shifting the subject.

"Not a word of that, for heaven's sake!" cried I. "If Cicero, traveling in the East, found sympathetic solace for his grief in beholding the arid overthrow of a once gorgeous city, shall not my petty affair be as nothing, when I behold in Hautboy the vine and the rose climbing the shattered shafts of his tumbled temple of Fame?"

Next day I tore all my manuscripts, bought me a fiddle, and went to take regular lessons of Hautboy.

POOR MAN'S PUDDING AND RICH MAN'S CRUMBS

PICTURE FIRST

Poor Man's Pudding

"You see," said poet Blandmour, enthusiastically—as some forty years ago we walked along the road in a soft, moist snowfall, toward the end of March—"you see, my friend, that the blessed almoner, Nature, is in all things beneficent; and not only so, but considerate in her charities, as any discreet human philanthropist might be. This snow, now, which seems so unseasonable, is in fact just what a poor husbandman needs. Rightly is this soft March snow, falling just before seed-time, rightly it is called 'Poor Man's Manure.' Distilling from kind heaven upon the soil, by a gentle penetration it nourishes every clod, ridge, and furrow. To the poor farmer it is as good as the rich farmer's farmyard enrichments. And the poor man has no trouble to spread it, while the rich man has to spread his."

"Perhaps so," said I, without equal enthusiasm, brushing some of the damp flakes from my chest. "It may be as you say, dear Blandmour. But tell me, how is it that the wind drives yonder drifts of 'Poor Man's Manure' off poor Coulter's two-acre patch here, and piles it up yonder on rich Squire Teamster's twenty-acre field?"

"Ah! to be sure—yes—well; Coulter's field, I suppose is sufficiently moist without further moistenings. Enough is as good as a feast, you know."

"Yes," replied I, "of this sort of damp fare," shaking another shower of the damp flakes from my person. "But tell me, this warm spring snow may answer very well, as you say; but how is it with the cold snows of the long, long winters here?"

"Why, do you not remember the words of the Psalmist?—'The Lord giveth snow like wool'; meaning not only that snow is white as wool, but warm, too, as wool. For the only reason, as I take it, that wool is comfortable, is because air is entangled, and therefore warmed among its fibres. Just so, then, take the temperature of a December field when covered with this snow-fleece, and you will no doubt find it several degrees above that of the air. So, you see, the winter's snow *itself* is beneficent; under the pretense of frost—a sort of gruff philanthropist—actually warming the earth, which afterward is to be fertilizingly moistened by these gentle flakes of March."

"I like to hear you talk, dear Blandmour; and, guided by your benevolent heart, can only wish to poor Coulter plenty of this 'Poor Man's Manure.'"

"But that is not all," said Blandmour, eagerly. "Did you never hear of the 'Poor Man's Eye-water'?"

"Never."

"Take this soft March snow, melt it, and bottle it. It keeps pure as alcohol. The very best thing in the world for weak eyes. I have a whole demijohn of it myself. But the poorest man, afflicted in his eyes, can freely help himself to this same all-bountiful remedy. Now, what a kind provision is that!"

"Then 'Poor Man's Manure' is 'Poor Man's Eye-water' too?"

"Exactly. And what could be more economically contrived? One thing answering two ends—ends so very distinct."

"Very distinct, indeed."

"Ah! that is your way. Making sport of earnest. But never mind. We have been talking of snow; but common rain-water—such as falls all the year round—is still more kindly. Not to speak of its known fertilizing quality as to fields, consider it in one of its minor lights. Pray, did you ever hear of a 'Poor Man's Egg'?"

"Never. What is that, now?"

"Why, in making some culinary preparations of meal and flour, where eggs are recommended in the receipt-book, a substitute for the eggs may be had in a cup of cold rain-water, which acts as leaven. And so a cup of cold rain-water thus used is called by housewives a 'Poor Man's Egg.' And many rich men's housekeepers sometimes use it."

"But only when they are out of hen's eggs, I presume, dear Blandmour. But your talk is—I sincerely say it—most agreeable to me. Talk on."

"Then there's 'Poor Man's Plaster' for wounds and other bodily harms; an alleviative and curative, compounded of simple, natural things; and so, being very cheap, is accessible to the poorest sufferers. Rich men often use 'Poor Man's Plaster'."

"But not without the judicious advice of a fee'd physician, dear Blandmour."

"Doubtless, they first consult the physician; but that may be an unnecessary precaution."

"Perhaps so. I do not gainsay it. Go on."

"Well, then, did you ever eat of a 'Poor Man's Pudding'?"

"I never so much as heard of it before."

"Indeed! Well, now you shall eat of one; and you shall eat it, too, as made, unprompted, by a poor man's wife, and you shall eat it at a poor man's table, and in a poor man's house. Come now, and if after this eating, you do not say that a 'Poor Man's Pudding' is as relishable as a rich man's, I will give up the point altogether; which briefly is: that, through kind Nature, the poor, out of their very poverty, extract comfort."

Not to narrate any more of our conversations upon this subject (for we had several—I being at that time the guest of Blandmour in the country, for the benefit of my health), suffice it that acting upon Blandmour's hint, I introduced myself into Coulter's house on a wet Monday noon (for the snow had thawed), under the innocent pretense of craving a pedestrian's rest and refreshment for an hour or two.

I was greeted, not without much embarrassment—owing, I suppose to my dress—but still with unaffected and honest kindness. Dame Coulter was just leaving the wash-tub to get ready her one o'clock meal against her good man's return from a deep wood about a mile distant among the hills, where he was chopping by day's work—seventy-five cents per day and found himself. The washing being done outside the main building, under an infirm-looking old shed, the dame stood upon a half-rotten soaked board to protect her feet, as well as might be, from the penetrating damp of the bare ground; hence she looked pale and chill. But her paleness had still another and more secret cause—the paleness of a mother to be. A quiet, fathomless heart-trouble, too, couched beneath the mild, resigned blue of her soft and wife-like eye. But she smiled upon me, as apologizing for the unavoidable disorder of a Monday and a washing-day, and, conducting me into the kitchen, set me down in the best seat it had—an old-fashioned chair of an enfeebled constitution.

I thanked her; and sat rubbing my hands before the ineffectual low fire, and—unobservantly as I could—glancing now and then about the room, while the good woman, throwing on more sticks said she was sorry the room was no warmer. Something more she said, too—not repiningly, however—of the fuel, as old and damp; picked-up sticks in Squire Teamster's forest, where her husband was chopping the sappy logs of the living tree for the Squire's fires. It needed not her remark, whatever it was, to convince me of the inferior quality of the sticks; some being quite mossy and toadstooled with long lying bedded among the accumulated dead leaves of many autumns. They made a sad hissing, and vain spluttering enough.

"You must rest yourself here till dinner-time, at least," said the dame; "what I have you are heartily welcome to."

I thanked her again, and begged her not to heed my presence in the least, but go on with her usual affairs.

I was struck by the aspect of the room. The house was old, and constitutionally damp. The window-sills had beads of exuded dampness upon them. The shriveled sashes shook in their frames, and the green panes of glass were clouded with the long thaw. On some little errand the dame passed into an adjoining chamber, leaving the door partly open. The floor of that room was carpetless, as the kitchen's was. Nothing but bare necessaries were about me; and those not of the best sort. Not a print on the wall but an old volume of Doddridge lay on the smoked chimney-shelf.

"You must have walked a long way, sir; you sigh so with weariness."

"No, I am not nigh so weary as yourself, I dare say."

"Oh, but I am accustomed to that; *you* are not, I should think," and her soft, sad blue eye ran over my dress. "But I must sweep these shavings away; husband made him a new ax-helve this morning before sunrise, and I have been so busy washing, that I have had no time to clear up. But now they are just the thing I want for the fire. They'd be much better though, were they not so green."

Now if Blandmour were here, thought I to myself, he would call those green shavings "Poor Man's Matches," or "Poor Man's Tinder," or some pleasant name of that sort.

"I do not know," said the good woman, turning round to me again—as she stirred among her pots on the smoky fire—"I do not know how you will like our pudding. It is only rice, milk, and salt boiled together."

"Ah, what they call 'Poor Man's Pudding,' I suppose you mean?"

A quick flush, half resentful, passed over her face.

"We do not call it so, sir," she said, and was silent.

Upbraiding myself for my inadvertence, I could not but again think to myself what Blandmour would have said, had he heard those words and seen that flush.

At last a slow, heavy footfall was heard; then a scraping at the door, and another voice said, "Come, wife; come, come—I must be back again in a jif—if you say I *must* take all my meals at home, you must be speedy; because the Squire—Good-day, sir," he exclaimed, now first catching sight of me as he entered the room. He turned toward his wife, inquiringly, and stood stock-still, while the moisture oozed from his patched boots to the floor.

"This gentleman stops here awhile to rest and refresh: he will take dinner with us, too. All will be ready now in a trice: so sit down on the bench, husband, and be patient, I pray. You see, sir," she continued, turning to me, "William there wants, of mornings, to carry a cold meal into the woods with him, to save the long one-o'clock walk across the fields to and fro. But I won't let him. A warm dinner is more than pay for the long walk."

"I don't know about that," said William, shaking his head. "I have often debated in my mind whether it really paid. There's not much odds, either way, between a wet walk after hard work, and a wet dinner before it. But I like to oblige a good wife like Martha. And you know, sir, that women will have their whimseys."

"I wish they all had as kind whimseys as your wife has," said I.

"Well, I've heard that some women ain't all maple-sugar; but, content with dear Martha, I don't know much about others."

"You find rare wisdom in the woods," mused I.

"Now, husband, if you ain't too tired, just lend a hand to draw the table out."

"Nay," said I; "let him rest, and let me help."

"No," said William, rising.

"Sit still," said his wife to me.

The table set, in due time we all found ourselves with plates before us.

"You see what we have," said Coulter—"salt pork, rye-bread, and pudding. Let me help you. I got this pork of the Squire; some of his last year's pork, which he let me have on account. It isn't quite as sweet as this year's would be; but I find it hearty enough to work on, and that's all I eat for. Only let the rheumatiz and other sicknesses keep clear of me, and I ask no flavors or favors from any. But you don't eat of the pork!"

"I see," said the wife, gently and gravely, "that the gentleman knows the difference between this year's and last year's pork. But perhaps he will like the pudding."

I summoned up all my self-control, and smilingly assented to the proposition of the pudding, without by my looks casting any reflections upon the pork. But, to tell the truth, it was quite impossible for me (not being ravenous, but only a little hungry at that time) to eat of the latter. It had a yellowish crust all round it, and was rather rankish, I thought, to the taste. I observed, too, that the dame did not eat of it, though she suffered some to be put on her plate, and pretended to be busy with it when Coulter looked that way. But she ate of the rye-bread, and so did I.

"Now, then, for the pudding," said Coulter. "Quick, wife; the Squire sits in his sitting-room window, looking far out across the fields. His timepiece is true."

"He don't play the spy on you, does he?" said I.

"Oh, no!—I don't say that. He's a good enough man. He gives me work. But he's particular. Wife, help the gentleman. You see, sir, if I lose the Squire's work, what will become of—" and, with a look for which I honored humanity, with sly significance, he glanced toward his wife; then, a little changing his voice, instantly continued—"that fine horse I am going to buy?"

"I guess," said the dame, with a strange, subdued sort of inefficient pleasantry—"I guess that fine horse you sometimes so merrily dream of will long stay in the Squire's stall. But sometimes his man gives me a Sunday ride."

"A Sunday ride!" said I.

"You see," resumed Coulter, "wife loves to go to church; but the nighest is four miles off, over yon snowy hills. So she can't walk it; and I can't carry her in my arms, though I have carried her up-stairs before now. But, as she says, the Squire's man sometimes gives her a lift on the road; and for this cause it is that I speak of a horse I am going to have one of these fine sunny days. And already, before having it, I have christened it 'Martha.' But what am I about? Come, come, wife! The pudding! Help the gentleman, do! The Squire! the Squire!—think of the Squire! and help round the pudding. There, one—two—three mouthfuls must do me. Good-by, wife. Good-by, sir, I'm off."

And, snatching his soaked hat, the noble Poor Man hurriedly went out into the soak and the mire.

I suppose now, thinks I to myself, that Blandmour would poetically say, He goes to take a Poor Man's saunter.

"You have a fine husband," said I to the woman, as we were now left together.

"William loves me this day as on the wedding-day, sir. Some hasty words, but never a harsh one. I wish I were better and stronger for his sake. And, oh! sir, both for his sake and mine" (and the soft, blue, beautiful eyes turned into two well-springs), "how I wish little William and Martha lived—it is so lonely-like now. William named after him, and Martha for me."

When a companion's heart of itself overflows, the best one can do is to do nothing. I sat looking down on my as yet untasted pudding.

"You should have seen little William, sir. Such a bright, manly boy, only six years old—cold, cold now!"

Plunging my spoon into the pudding, I forced some into my mouth to stop it.

"And little Martha—Oh! sir, she was the beauty! Bitter, bitter! but needs must be borne!"

The mouthful of pudding now touched my palate, and touched it with a mouldy, briny taste. The rice, I knew, was of that damaged sort sold cheap; and the salt from the last year's pork barrel.

"Ah, sir, if those little ones yet to enter the world were the same little ones which so sadly have left it; returning friends, not strangers, strangers, always strangers! Yet does a mother soon learn to love them; for certain, sir, they come from where the others have gone. Don't you believe that, sir? Yes, I know all good people must. But, still, still—and I fear it is wicked, and very black-hearted, too—still, strive how I may to cheer me with thinking of little William and Martha in heaven, and with reading Dr. Doddridge there—still, still does dark grief leak in, just like the rain through our roof. I am left so lonesome now; day after day, all the day long, dear William is gone; and all the damp day long grief drizzles and drizzles down on my soul. But I pray to God to forgive me for this; and for the rest, manage it as well as I may."

Bitter and mouldy is the "Poor Man's Pudding," groaned I to myself, half choked with but one little mouthful of it, which would hardly go down.

I could stay no longer to hear of sorrows for which the sincerest sympathies could give no adequate relief; of a fond persuasion, to which there could be furnished no further proof than already was had—a persuasion, too, of that sort which much speaking is sure more or less to mar; of causeless self-upbraidings, which no expostulations could have dispelled, I offered no pay for hospitalities gratuitous and honorable as those of a prince. I knew that such offerings would have been more than declined; charity resented.

The native American poor never lose their delicacy or pride; hence, though unreduced to the physical degradation of the European pauper, they yet suffer more in mind than the poor of any other people in the world. Those peculiar social sensibilities nourished by our peculiar political principles, while they enhance the true dignity of a prosperous American, do but minister to the added wretchedness of the unfortunate; first, by prohibiting their acceptance of what little random relief charity may offer; and, second, by furnishing them with the keenest appreciation of the smarting distinction between their ideal of universal equality and their grindstone experience of the practical misery and infamy of poverty—a misery and infamy which is, ever has been, and ever will be, precisely the same in India, England, and America.

Under pretense that my journey called me forthwith, I bade the dame good-by; shook her cold hand; looked my last into her blue, resigned eye, and went out into the wet. But cheerless as it was, and damp, damp, damp—the heavy atmosphere charged with all sorts of incipiencies—I yet became conscious by the suddenness of the contrast, that the house air I had quitted was laden down with that peculiar deleterious quality, the height of which—insufferable to some visitants—will be found in a poorhouse ward.

This ill-ventilation in winter of the rooms of the poor—a thing, too, so stubbornly persisted in—is usually charged upon them as their disgraceful neglect of the most simple means to health. But the instinct of the poor is wiser than we think. The air which ventilates, likewise *cools*. And to any shiverer, ill-ventilated warmth is better than well-ventilated cold. Of all the preposterous assumptions of humanity over humanity, nothing exceeds most of the criticisms made on the habits of the poor by the well-housed, well-warmed, and well-fed.

"Blandmour," said I that evening, as after tea I sat on his comfortable sofa, before a blazing fire, with one of his two ruddy little children on my knee, "you are not what may rightly be called a rich man; you have a fair competence; no more. Is it not so? Well then, I do not include *you*, when I say, that if ever a rich man speaks prosperously to me of a Poor Man, I shall set it down as—I won't mention the word."

PICTURE SECOND

Rich Man's Crumbs

In the year 1814, during the summer following my first taste of the "Poor Man's Pudding," a sea-voyage was recommended to me by my physician. The Battle of Waterloo having closed the long drama of Napoleon's wars, many strangers were visiting Europe. I arrived in London at the time the victorious princes were there assembled enjoying the Arabian Nights' hospitalities of a grateful and gorgeous aristocracy, and the courtliest of gentlemen and kings—George the Prince Regent.

I had declined all letters but one to my banker. I wandered about for the best reception an adventurous traveler can have—the reception I mean, which unsolicited chance and accident throw in his venturous way.

But I omit all else to recount one hour's hap under the lead of a very friendly man, whose acquaintance I made in the open street of Cheapside. He wore a uniform, and was some sort of a civic subordinate; I forget exactly what. He was off duty that day. His discourse was chiefly of the noble charities of London. He took me to two or three, and made admiring mention of many more.

"But," said he, as we turned into Cheapside again, "if you are at all curious about such things, let me take you—if it be not too late—to one of the most interesting of all—our Lord Mayor's Charities, sir; nay, the charities not only of a Lord Mayor, but, I may truly say, in this one instance, of emperors, regents, and kings. You remember the event of yesterday?"

"That sad fire on the river-side, you mean, unhousing so many of the poor?"

"No. The grand Guildhall Banquet to the princes. Who can forget it? Sir, the dinner was served on nothing but solid silver and gold plate, worth at the least £200,000—that is, 1,000,000 of your dollars; while the mere expenditure of meats, wines, attendance and upholstery, etc., can not be footed under £25,000—120,000 dollars of your hard cash."

"But, surely, my friend, you do not call that charity—feeding kings at that rate?"

"No. The feast came first—yesterday; and the charity after—to-day. How else would you have it, where princes are concerned? But I think we shall be quite in time—come; here we are at King Street, and down there is Guildhall. Will you go?"

"Gladly, my good friend. Take me where you will. I come but to roam and see."

Avoiding the main entrance of the hall, which was barred, he took me through some private way, and we found ourselves in a rear blind-walled place in the open air. I looked round amazed. The spot was grimy as a backyard in the Five Points. It was packed with a mass of lean, famished, ferocious creatures, struggling and fighting for some mysterious precedency, and all holding soiled blue tickets in their hands.

"There is no other way," said my guide; "we can only get in with the crowd. Will you try it? I hope you have not on your drawing-room suit? What do you say? It will be well worth your sight. So noble a charity does not often offer. The one following the annual banquet of Lord Mayor's day—fine a charity as that certainly is—is not to be mentioned with what will be seen to-day. Is it, ay?"

As he spoke, a basement door in the distance was thrown open, and the squalid mass made a rush for the dark vault beyond.

I nodded to my guide, and sideways we joined in with the rest. Ere long we found our retreat cut off by the yelping crowd behind, and I could not but congratulate myself on having a civic, as well as civil guide; one, too, whose uniform made evident his authority.

It was just the same as if I were pressed by a mob of cannibals on some pagan beach. The beings round me roared with famine. For in this mighty London misery but maddens. In the country it softens. As I gazed on the meagre, murderous pack, I thought of the blue eye of the gentle wife of poor Coulter. Some sort of curved, glittering steel thing (not a sword; I know not what it was), before worn in his belt, was now flourished overhead by my guide, menacing the creatures to forbear offering the stranger violence.

As we drove, slow and wedge-like, into the gloomy vault, the howls of the mass reverberated. I seemed seething in the Pit with the Lost. On and on, through the dark and damp, and then up a stone stairway to a wide portal; when, diffusing, the pestiferous mob poured in bright day between painted walls and beneath a painted dome. I thought of the anarchic sack of Versailles.

A few moments more and I stood bewildered among the beggars in the famous Guildhall.

Where I stood—where the thronged rabble stood, less than twelve hours before sat His Imperial Majesty, Alexander of Russia; His Royal Majesty, Frederick William, King of Prussia; His Royal Highness, George,

Prince Regent of England; His world-renowned Grace, the Duke of Wellington; with a mob of magnificoes, made up of conquering field marshals, earls, counts, and innumerable other nobles of mark.

The walls swept to and fro, like the foliage of a forest with blazonings of conquerors' flags. Naught outside the hall was visible. No windows were within four-and-twenty feet of the floor. Cut off from all other sights, I was hemmed in by one splendid spectacle—splendid, I mean, everywhere, but as the eye fell toward the floor. *That* was foul as a hovel's—as a kennel's; the naked boards being strewed with the smaller and more wasteful fragments of the feast, while the two long parallel lines, up and down the hall, of now unrobed, shabby, dirty pine-tables were piled with less trampled wrecks. The dyed banners were in keeping with the last night's kings: the floor suited the beggars of to-day. The banners looked upon the floor as from his balcony Dives upon Lazarus. A line of liveried men kept back with their staves the impatient jam of the mob, who, otherwise, might have instantaneously converted the Charity into a Pillage. Another body of gowned and gilded officials distributed the broken meats—the cold victuals and crumbs of kings. One after another the beggars held up their dirty blue tickets, and were served with the plundered wreck of a pheasant, or the rim of a pasty—like the detached crown of an old hat—the solids and meats stolen out.

"What a noble charity," whispered my guide. "See that pasty now, snatched by that pale girl; I dare say the Emperor of Russia ate of that last night."

"Very probably," murmured I; "it looks as though some omnivorous emperor or other had had a finger in that pie."

"And see yon pheasant too—there—that one—the boy in the torn shirt has it now—look! The Prince Regent might have dined off that."

The two breasts were gouged ruthlessly out, exposing the bare bones, embellished with the untouched pinions and legs.

"Yes, who knows!" said my guide, "his Royal Highness the Prince Regent might have eaten of that identical pheasant."

"I don't doubt it," murmured I, "he is said to be uncommonly fond of the breast. But where is Napoleon's head in a charger? I should fancy that ought to have been the principal dish."

"You are merry. Sir, even Cossacks are charitable here in Guildhall. Look! the famous Platoff, the Hetman himself—(he was here last night with the rest)—no doubt he thrust a lance into yon pork-pie there. Look! the old shirtless man has it now. How he licks his chops over it, little thinking of or thanking the good, kind Cossack that left it him! Ah! another—a stouter has grabbed it. It falls; bless my soul!—the dish is quite empty—only a bit of the hacked crust."

"The Cossacks, my friend, are said to be immoderately fond of fat," observed I. "The Hetman was hardly so charitable as you thought."

"A noble charity, upon the whole, for all that. See, even Gog and Magog yonder, at the other end of the hall fairly laugh out their delight at the scene."

"But don't you think, though," hinted I, "that the sculptor, whoever he was, carved the laugh too much into a grin—a sort of sardonical grin?"

"Well, that's as you take it, sir. But see—now I'd wager a guinea the Lord Mayor's lady dipped her golden spoon into yonder golden-hued jelly. See, the jelly-eyed old body has slipped it, in one broad gulp, down his throat."

"Peace to that jelly!" breathed I.

"What a generous, noble, magnanimous charity this is! unheard of in any country but England, which feeds her very beggars with golden-hued jellies."

"But not three times every day, my friend. And do you really think that jellies are the best sort of relief you can furnish to beggars? Would not plain beef and bread, with something to do, and be paid for, be better?"

"But plain beef and bread were not eaten here. Emperors, and prince-regents, and kings, and field marshals don't often dine on plain beef and bread. So the leavings are according. Tell me, can you expect that the crumbs of kings can be like the crumbs of squirrels?"

"*You!* I mean *you*! stand aside, or else be served and away! Here, take this pasty, and be thankful that you taste of the same dish with her Grace the Duchess of Devonshire. Graceless ragamuffin, do you hear?"

These words were bellowed at me through the din by a red-gowned official nigh the board.

"Surely he does not mean *me*," said I to my guide; "he has not confounded *me* with the rest."

"One is known by the company he keeps," smiled my guide. "See! not only stands your hat awry and bunged on your head, but your coat is fouled and torn. Nay," he cried to the red-gown, "this is an unfortunate friend: a simple spectator, I assure you."

"Ah! is that you, old lad?" responded the red-gown, in familiar recognition of my guide—a personal friend as it seemed; "well, convey your friend out forthwith. Mind the grand crash; it will soon be coming; hark! now! away with him!"

Too late. The last dish had been seized. The yet unglutted mob raised a fierce yell, which wafted the banners like a strong gust, and filled the air with a reek as from sewers. They surged against the tables, broke through all barriers, and billowed over the hall—their bare tossed arms like the dashed ribs of a wreck. It seemed to me as if a sudden impotent fury of fell envy possessed them. That one half-hour's peep at the mere remnants of the glories of the Banquets of Kings; the unsatisfying mouthfuls of disemboweled pasties, plundered pheasants, and half-sucked jellies, served to remind them of the intrinsic contempt of the alms. In this sudden mood, or whatever mysterious thing it was that now seized them, these Lazaruses seemed ready to spew up in repentant scorn the contumelious crumbs of Dives.

"This way, this way! stick like a bee to my back," intensely whispered my guide. "My friend there has answered my beck, and thrown open yon private door for us two. Wedge—wedge in—quick, there goes your bunged hat—never stop for your coat-tail—hit that man—strike him down! hold! jam! now! wrench along for your life! ha! here we breathe freely; thank God! You faint. Ho!"

"Never mind. This fresh air revives me."

I inhaled a few more breaths of it, and felt ready to proceed.

"And now conduct me, my good friend, by some front passage into Cheapside, forthwith. I must home."

"Not by the sidewalk though. Look at your dress. I must get a hack for you."

"Yes, I suppose so," said I, ruefully eyeing my tatters, and then glancing in envy at the close-buttoned coat and flat cap of my guide, which defied all tumblings and tearings.

"There, now, sir," said the honest fellow, as he put me into the hack, and tucked in me and my rags, "when you get back to your own country, you can say you have witnessed the greatest of all England's noble charities. Of course, you will make reasonable allowances for the unavoidable jam. Good-by. Mind, Jehu"—addressing the driver on the box—"this is a *gentleman* you carry. He is just from the Guildhall Charity, which accounts for his appearance. Go on now. London Tavern, Fleet Street, remember, is the place."

"Now, Heaven in its kind mercy save me from the noble charities of London," sighed I, as that night I lay bruised and battered on my bed; "and Heaven save me equally from the 'Poor Man's Pudding' and the 'Rich Man's Crumbs.'"

THE HAPPY FAILURE

A STORY OF THE RIVER HUDSON

The appointment was that I should meet my elderly uncle at the riverside, precisely at nine in the morning. The skiff was to be ready, and the apparatus to be brought down by his grizzled old black man. As yet, the nature of the wonderful experiment remained a mystery to all but the projector.

I was first on the spot. The village was high up the river, and the inland summer sun was already oppressively warm. Presently I saw my uncle advancing beneath the trees, hat off, and wiping his brow; while far behind struggled poor old Yorpy, with what seemed one of the gates of Gaza on his back.

"Come, hurrah, stump along, Yorpy!" cried my uncle, impatiently turning round every now and then.

Upon the black's staggering up to the skiff, I perceived that the great gate of Gaza was transformed into a huge, shabby, oblong box, hermetically sealed. The sphinx-like blankness of the box quadrupled the mystery in my mind.

"Is *this* the wonderful apparatus," said I in amazement. "Why, it's nothing but a battered old dry-goods box, nailed up. And is *this* the thing, uncle, that is to make you a million of dollars ere the year be out? What a forlorn-looking, lack-lustre, old ash-box it is."

"Put it into the skiff!" roared my uncle to Yorpy, without heeding my boyish disdain. "Put it in, you grizzled-headed cherub—put it in carefully, carefully! If that box bursts, my everlasting fortune collapses."

"Bursts?—collapses?" cried I, in alarm. "It ain't full of combustibles? Quick, let me go to the further end of the boat!"

"Sit still, you simpleton!" cried my uncle again. "Jump in, Yorpy, and hold on to the box like grim death while I shove off. Carefully! carefully! you dunderheaded black! Mind t'other side of the box, I say! Do you mean to destroy the box?"

"Duyvel take te pox!" muttered old Yorpy, who was a sort of Dutch African. "De pox has been my cuss for de ten long 'ear."

"Now, then, we're off—take an oar, youngster; you, Yorpy, clinch the box fast. Here we go now. Carefully! carefully! You, Yorpy, stop shaking the box! Easy! there's a big snag. Pull now. Hurrah! deep water at last! Now give way, youngster, and away to the island."

"The island!" said I. "There's no island hereabouts."

"There is ten miles above the bridge, though," said my uncle, determinately.

"Ten miles off! Pull that old dry-goods box ten miles up the river in this blazing sun?"

"All that I have to say," said my uncle, firmly, "is that we are bound to Quash Island."

"Mercy, uncle! if I had known of this great long pull of ten mortal miles in this fiery sun, you wouldn't have juggled *me* into the skiff so easy. What's *in* that box?—paving-stones? See how the skiff settles down under it. I won't help pull a box of paving-stones ten miles. What's the use of pulling 'em?"

"Look you, simpleton," quoth my uncle, pausing upon his suspended oar. "Stop rowing, will ye! Now then, if you don't want to share in the glory of my experiment; if you are wholly indifferent to halving its immortal renown; I say, sir, if you care not to be present at the first trial of my Great Hydraulic-Hydrostatic Apparatus for draining swamps and marshes, and converting them, at the rate of one acre the hour, into fields more fertile than those of the Genesee; if you care not, I repeat, to have this proud thing to tell—in far future days, when poor old I shall have been long dead and gone, boy—to your children and your children's children; in that case, sir, you are free to land forthwith."

"Oh, uncle! I did not mean—"

"No words, sir! Yorpy, take his oar, and help pull him ashore."

"But, my dear uncle; I declare to you that—"

"Not a syllable, sir; you have cast open scorn upon the Great Hydraulic-Hydrostatic Apparatus. Yorpy, put him ashore, Yorpy. It's shallow here again. Jump out, Yorpy, and wade with him ashore."

"Now, my dear, good, kind uncle, do but pardon me this one time, and I will say nothing about the apparatus."

"Say nothing about it! when it is my express end and aim it shall be famous! Put him ashore, Yorpy."

"Nay, uncle, I *will* not give up my oar. I have an oar in this matter, and I mean to keep it. You shall not cheat me out my share of your glory."

"Ah, now there—that's sensible. You may stay, youngster. Pull again now."

We were all silent for a time, steadily plying our way. At last I ventured to break water once more.

"I am glad, dear uncle, you have revealed to me at last the nature and end of your great experiment. It is the effectual draining of swamps; an attempt, dear uncle, in which, if you do but succeed (as I know you will), you will earn the glory denied to a Roman emperor. He tried to drain the Pontine marsh, but failed."

"The world has shot ahead the length of its own diameter since then," quoth my uncle, proudly. "If that Roman emperor were here, I'd show him what can be done in the present enlightened age."

Seeing my good uncle so far mollified now as to be quite self-complacent, I ventured another remark.

"This is a rather severe, hot pull, dear uncle."

"Glory is not to be gained, youngster, without pulling hard for it—against the stream, too, as we do now. The natural tendency of man, in the mass, is to go down with the universal current into oblivion."

"But why pull so far, dear uncle, upon the present occasion? Why pull ten miles for it? You do but propose, as I understand it, to put to the actual test this admirable invention of yours. And could it not be tested almost anywhere?"

"Simple boy," quoth my uncle, "would you have some malignant spy steal from me the fruits of ten long years of high-hearted, persevering endeavor? Solitary in my scheme, I go to a solitary place to test it. If I fail—for all things are possible—no one out of the family will know it. If I succeed, secure in the secrecy of my invention, I can boldly demand any price for its publication."

"Pardon me, dear uncle; you are wiser than I."

"One would think years and gray hairs should bring wisdom, boy."

"Yorpy there, dear uncle; think you his grizzled locks thatch a brain improved by long life?"

"Am I Yorpy, boy? Keep to your oar!"

Thus padlocked again, I said no further word till the skiff grounded on the shallows, some twenty yards from the deep-wooded isle.

"Hush!" whispered my uncle, intensely; "not a word now!" and he sat perfectly still, slowly sweeping with his glance the whole country around, even to both banks of the here wide-expanded stream.

"Wait till that horseman, yonder, passes!" he whispered again, pointing to a speck moving along a lofty, riverside road, which perilously wound on midway up a long line of broken bluffs and cliffs. "There— he's out of sight now, behind the copse. Quick! Yorpy! Carefully, though! Jump overboard, and shoulder the box, and—Hold!"

We were all mute and motionless again.

"Ain't that a boy, sitting like Zaccheus in yonder tree of the orchard on the other bank? Look, youngster—young eyes are better than old—don't you see him?"

"Dear uncle, I see the orchard, but I can't see any boy."

"He's a spy—I know he is," suddenly said my uncle, disregardful of my answer, and intently gazing, shading his eyes with his flattened hand. "Don't touch the box, Yorpy. Crouch! crouch down, all of ye!"

"Why, uncle—there—see—the boy is only a withered white bough. I see it very plainly now."

"You don't see the tree I mean," quoth my uncle, with a decided air of relief, "but never mind; I defy the boy. Yorpy, jump out, and shoulder the box. And now then, youngster, off with your shoes and stockings, roll up your trousers legs, and follow me. Carefully, Yorpy, carefully. That's more precious than a box of gold, mind."

"Heavy as de gelt anyhow," growled Yorpy, staggering and splashing in the shallows beneath it.

"There, stop under the bushes there—in among the flags—so—gently, gently—there, put it down just there. Now youngster, are you ready? Follow—tiptoes, tiptoes!"

"I can't wade in this mud and water on my tiptoes, uncle; and I don't see the need of it either."

"Go ashore, sir—instantly!"

"Why, uncle, I *am* ashore."

"Peace! follow me, and no more."

Crouching in the water in complete secrecy, beneath the bushes and among the tall flags, my uncle now stealthily produced a hammer and wrench from one of his enormous pockets, and presently tapped the box. But the sound alarmed him.

"Yorpy," he whispered, "go you off to the right, behind the bushes, and keep watch. If you see any one coming, whistle softly. Youngster, you do the same to the left."

We obeyed; and presently, after considerable hammering and supplemental tinkering, my uncle's voice was heard in the utter solitude, loudly commanding our return.

Again we obeyed, and now found the cover of the box removed. All eagerness, I peeped in, and saw a surprising multiplicity of convoluted metal pipes and syringes of all sorts and varieties, all sizes and calibres, inextricably interwreathed together in one gigantic coil. It looked like a huge nest of anacondas and adders.

"Now then, Yorpy," said my uncle, all animation, and flushed with the foretaste of glory, "do you stand this side, and be ready to tip when I give the word. And do you, youngster, stand ready to do as much for the other side. Mind, don't budge it the fraction of a barley-corn till I say the word. All depends on a proper adjustment."

"No fear, uncle. I will be careful as a lady's tweezers."

"I s'ant life de heavy pox," growled old Yorpy, "till de wort pe given; no fear o' dat."

"Oh, boy," said my uncle now, upturning his face devotionally, while a really noble gleam irradiated his gray eyes, locks, and wrinkles; "Oh, boy! this, *this* is the hour which for ten long years has, in the prospect, sustained me through all my painstaking obscurity. Fame will be the sweeter because it comes at the last; the truer, because it comes to an old man like me, not to a boy like you. Sustainer! I glorify Thee."

He bowed over his venerable head, and—as I live—something like a shower-drop somehow fell from my face into the shallows.

"Tip!"

We tipped.

"A *leetle* more!"

We tipped a little more.

"A *leetle* more!"

We tipped a *leetle* more.

"Just a *leetle*, very *leetle* bit more."

With great difficulty we tipped just a *leetle*, very *leetle* more.

All this time my uncle was diligently stooping over, and striving to peep in, up, and under the box where the coiled anacondas and adders lay; but the machine being now fairly immersed, the attempt was wholly vain.

He rose erect, and waded slowly all round the box; his countenance firm and reliant, but not a little troubled and vexed.

It was plain something or other was going wrong. But as I was left in utter ignorance as to the mystery of the contrivance, I could not tell where the difficulty lay, or what was the proper remedy.

Once more, still more slowly, still more vexedly, my uncle waded round the box, the dissatisfaction gradually deepening, but still controlled, and still with hope at the bottom of it.

Nothing could be more sure than that some anticipated effect had, as yet, failed to develop itself. Certain I was, too, that the water-line did not lower about my legs.

"Tip it a *leetle* bit—very *leetle* now."

"Dear uncle, it is tipped already as far as it can be. Don't you see it rests now square on its bottom?"

"You, Yorpy, take your black hoof from under the box!"

This gust of passion on the part of my uncle made the matter seem still more dubious and dark. It was a bad symptom, I thought.

"Surely you *can* tip it just a *leetle* more!"

"Not a hair, uncle."

"Blast and blister the cursed box then!" roared my uncle, in a terrific voice, sudden as a squall. Running at the box, he dashed his bare foot into it, and with astonishing power all but crushed in the side. Then seizing the whole box, he disemboweled it of all its anacondas and adders, and, tearing and wrenching them, flung them right and left over the water.

"Hold, hold, my dear, dear uncle!—do for heaven's sake desist. Don't destroy so, in one frantic moment, all your long calm years of devotion to one darling scheme. Hold, I conjure!"

Moved by my vehement voice and uncontrollable tears, he paused in his work of destruction, and stood steadfastly eyeing me, or rather blankly staring at me, like one demented.

"It is not yet wholly ruined, dear uncle; come put it together now. You have hammer and wrench; put it together again, and try it once more. While there is life there is hope."

"While there is life hereafter there is *despair*," he howled.

"Do, do now, dear uncle—here, here, put those pieces together; or, if that can't be done without more tools, try a *section* of it—that will do just as well. Try it once; try, uncle."

My persistent persuasiveness told upon him. The stubborn stump of hope, plowed at and uprooted in vain, put forth one last miraculous green sprout.

Steadily and carefully pulling out of the wreck some of the more curious-looking fragments, he mysteriously involved them together, and then, clearing out the box, slowly inserted them there, and ranging Yorpy and me as before, bade us tip the box once again.

We did so; and as no perceptible effect yet followed, I was each moment looking for the previous command to tip the box over yet more, when, glancing into my uncle's face, I started aghast. It seemed pinched, shriveled into mouldy whiteness, like a mildewed grape. I dropped the box, and sprang toward him just in time to prevent his fall.

Leaving the woeful box where we had dropped it, Yorpy and I helped the old man into the skiff and silently pulled from Quash Isle.

How swiftly the current now swept us down! How hardly before had we striven to stem it! I thought of my poor uncle's saying, not an hour gone by, about the universal drift of the mass of humanity toward utter oblivion.

"Boy!" said my uncle at last, lifting his head. I looked at him earnestly, and was gladdened to see that the terrible blight of his face had almost departed.

"Boy, there's not much left in an old world for an old man to invent."

I said nothing.

"Boy, take my advice, and never try to invent anything but—happiness."

I said nothing.

"Boy, about ship, and pull back for the box."

"Dear uncle!"

"It will make a good wood-box, boy. And faithful old Yorpy can sell the old iron for tobacco-money."

"Dear massa! dear old massa! dat be very fust time in de ten long 'ear yoo hab mention kindly old Yorpy. I tank yoo, dear old massa; I tank yoo so kindly. Yoo is yourself agin in de ten long 'ear."

"Ay, long ears enough," sighed my uncle; "Esopian ears. But it's all over now. Boy, I'm glad I've failed. I say, boy, failure has made a good old man of me. It was horrible at first, but I'm glad I've failed. Praise be to God for the failure!"

His face kindled with a strange, rapt earnestness. I have never forgotten that look. If the event made my uncle a good old man as he called it, it made me a wise young one. Example did for me the work of experience.

When some years had gone by, and my dear old uncle began to fail, and, after peaceful days of autumnal content, was gathered gently to his fathers—faithful old Yorpy closing his eyes—as I took my last look at his venerable face, the pale resigned lips seemed to move. I seemed to hear again his deep, fervent cry—"Praise be to God for the failure!"

THE 'GEES

In relating to my friends various passages of my sea-goings I have at times had occasion to allude to that singular people the 'Gees, sometimes as casual acquaintances, sometimes as shipmates. Such allusions have been quite natural and easy. For instance, I have said *The two 'Gees*, just as another would say *The two Dutchmen*, or *The two Indians*. In fact, being myself so familiar with 'Gees, it seemed as if all the rest of the world must be. But not so. My auditors have opened their eyes as much as to say, "What under the sun is a 'Gee?" To enlighten them I have repeatedly had to interrupt myself and not without detriment to my stories. To remedy which inconvenience, a friend hinted the advisability of writing out some account of the 'Gees, and having it published. Such as they are, the following memoranda spring from that happy suggestion:

The word *'Gee* (*g* hard) is an abbreviation, by seamen, of *Portugee*, the corrupt form of *Portuguese*. As the name is a curtailment, so the race is a residuum. Some three centuries ago certain Portuguese convicts were sent as a colony to Fogo, one of the Cape de Verdes, off the northwest coast of Africa, an island previously stocked with an aboriginal race of negroes, ranking pretty high in civility, but rather low in stature and morals. In course of time, from the amalgamated generation all the likelier sort were drafted off as food for powder, and the ancestors of the since-called 'Gees were left as the *caput mortum*, or melancholy remainder.

Of all men seamen have strong prejudices, particularly in the matter of race. They are bigots here. But when a creature of inferior race lives among them, an inferior tar, there seems no bound to their disdain. Now, as ere long will be hinted, the 'Gee, though of an aquatic nature, does not, as regards higher qualifications, make the best of sailors. In short, by seamen the abbreviation 'Gee was hit upon in pure contumely; the degree of which may be partially inferred from this, that with them the primitive word Portugee itself is a reproach; so that 'Gee, being a subtle distillation from that word, stands, in point of relative intensity to it, as attar of roses does to rose-water. At times, when some crusty old sea-dog has his spleen more than unusually excited against some luckless blunderer of Fogo his shipmate, it is marvelous the prolongation of taunt into which he will spin out the one little exclamatory monosyllable Ge-e-e-e-e!

The Isle of Fogo, that is, "Fire Isle," was so called from its volcano, which, after throwing up an infinite deal of stones and ashes, finally threw up business altogether, from its broadcast bounteousness having become bankrupt. But thanks to the volcano's prodigality in its time, the soil of Fogo is such as may be found on a dusty day on a road newly macadamized. Cut off from farms and gardens, the staple food of the inhabitants is fish, at catching which they are expert. But none the less do they relish ship-biscuit, which, indeed, by most islanders, barbarous or semi-barbarous, is held a sort of lozenge.

In his best estate the 'Gee is rather small (he admits it) but, with some exceptions, hardy; capable of enduring extreme hard work, hard fare, or hard usage, as the case may be. In fact, upon a scientific view, there would seem a natural adaptability in the 'Gee to hard times generally. A theory not uncorroborated by his experiences; and furthermore, that kindly care of Nature in fitting him for them, something as for his hard rubs with a hardened world Fox the Quaker fitted himself, namely, in a tough leather suit from top to toe. In other words, the 'Gee is by no means of that exquisitely delicate sensibility expressed by the figurative adjective thin-skinned. His physicals and spirituals are in singular contrast. The 'Gee has a great appetite, but little imagination; a large eyeball, but small insight. Biscuit he crunches, but sentiment he eschews.

His complexion is hybrid; his hair ditto; his mouth disproportionally large, as compared with his stomach; his neck short; but his head round, compact, and betokening a solid understanding.

Like the negro, the 'Gee has a peculiar savor, but a different one—a sort of wild, marine, gamey savor, as in the sea-bird called haglet. Like venison, his flesh is firm but lean.

His teeth are what are called butter-teeth, strong, durable, square, and yellow. Among captains at a loss for better discourse during dull, rainy weather in the horse-latitudes, much debate has been had whether his teeth are intended for carnivorous or herbivorous purposes, or both conjoined. But as on his isle the 'Gee eats neither flesh nor grass, this inquiry would seem superfluous.

The native dress of the 'Gee is, like his name, compendious. His head being by nature well thatched, he wears no hat. Wont to wade much in the surf, he wears no shoes. He has a serviceably hard heel, a kick from which is by the judicious held almost as dangerous as one from a wild zebra.

Though for a long time back no stranger to the seafaring people of Portugal, the 'Gee, until a comparatively recent period, remained almost undreamed of by seafaring Americans. It is now some forty years since he first became known to certain masters of our Nantucket ships, who commenced the practice of touching at Fogo, on the outward passage, there to fill up vacancies among their crews arising from the short supply of men at home. By degrees the custom became pretty general, till now the 'Gee is found aboard of almost one whaler out of three. One reason why they are in request is this: An unsophisticated 'Gee coming on board a foreign ship never asks for wages. He comes for biscuit. He does not know what wages mean, unless cuffs and buffets be wages, of which sort he receives a liberal allowance, paid with great punctuality, besides perquisites of punches thrown in now and then. But for all this, some persons there are, and not unduly biassed by partiality to him either, who still insist that the 'Gee never gets his due.

His docile services being thus cheaply to be had, some captains will go the length of maintaining that 'Gee sailors are preferable, indeed every way, physically and intellectually, superior to American sailors—such captains complaining, and justly, that American sailors, if not decently treated, are apt to give serious trouble.

But even by their most ardent admirers it is not deemed prudent to sail a ship with none but 'Gees, at least if they chance to be all green hands, a green 'Gee being of all green things the greenest. Besides, owing to the clumsiness of their feet ere improved by practice in the rigging, green 'Gees are wont, in no inconsiderable numbers, to fall overboard the first dark, squally night; insomuch that when unreasonable owners insist with a captain against his will upon a green 'Gee crew fore and aft, he will ship twice as many 'Gees as he would have shipped of Americans, so as to provide for all contingencies.

The 'Gees are always ready to be shipped. Any day one may go to their isle, and on the showing of a coin of biscuit over the rail, may load down to the water's edge with them.

But though any number of 'Gees are ever ready to be shipped, still it is by no means well to take them as they come. There is a choice even in 'Gees.

Of course the 'Gee has his private nature as well as his public coat. To know 'Gees—to be a sound judge of 'Gees—one must study them, just as to know and be a judge of horses one must study horses. Simple as for the most part are both horse and 'Gee, in neither case can knowledge of the creature come by intuition. How unwise, then, in those ignorant young captains who, on their first voyage, will go and ship their 'Gees at Fogo without any preparatory information, or even so much as taking convenient advice from a 'Gee jockey. By a 'Gee jockey is meant a man well versed in 'Gees. Many a young captain has been thrown and badly hurt by a 'Gee of his own choosing. For notwithstanding the general docility of the 'Gee when green, it may be otherwise with him when ripe. Discreet captains won't have such a 'Gee. "Away with that ripe 'Gee!" they cry; "that smart 'Gee; that knowing 'Gee! Green 'Gees for me!"

For the benefit of inexperienced captains about to visit Fogo, the following may be given as the best way to test a 'Gee: Get square before him, at, say three paces, so that the eye, like a shot, may rake the 'Gee fore and aft, at one glance taking in his whole make and build—how he looks about the head, whether he carry it well; his ears, are they over-lengthy? How fares it in the withers? His legs, does the 'Gee stand strongly on them? His knees, any Belshazzar symptoms there? How stands it in the regions of the brisket, etc., etc.

Thus far bone and bottom. For the rest, draw close to, and put the centre of the pupil of your eye—put it, as it were, right into the 'Gee's eye—even as an eye-stone, gently, but firmly slip it in there, and then note what speck or beam of viciousness, if any, will be floated out.

All this and more must be done; and yet after all, the best judge may be deceived. But on no account should the shipper negotiate for his 'Gee with any middle-man, himself a 'Gee. Because such an one must be a knowing 'Gee, who will be sure to advise the green 'Gee what things to hide and what to display, to hit the skipper's fancy; which, of course, the knowing 'Gee supposes to lean toward as much physical and moral excellence as possible. The rashness of trusting to one of these middle-men was forcibly shown in the case of the 'Gee who by his countrymen was recommended to a New Bedford captain as one of the most agile 'Gees in Fogo. There he stood straight and stout, in a flowing pair of man-of-war's-man trousers, uncommonly well fitted out. True, he did not step around much at the time. But that was diffidence. Good. They shipped him. But at the first taking in of sail the 'Gee hung fire. Come to look, both trousers-legs were full of elephantiasis. It was a long sperm-whaling voyage. Useless as so much lumber, at every port prohibited from being dumped ashore, that elephantine 'Gee, ever crunching biscuit, for three weary years was trundled round the globe.

Grown wise by several similar experiences, old Captain Hosea Kean, of Nantucket, in shipping a 'Gee, at present manages matters thus: He lands at Fogo in the night; by secret means gains information where the likeliest 'Gee wanting to ship lodges; whereupon with a strong party he surprises all the friends and acquaintances of that 'Gee; putting them under guard with pistols at their heads; then creeps cautiously toward the 'Gee, now lying wholly unawares in his hut, quite relaxed from all possibility of displaying aught deceptive in his appearance. Thus silently, thus suddenly, thus unannounced, Captain Kean bursts upon his 'Gee, so to speak, in the very bosom of his family. By this means, more than once, unexpected revelations have been made. A 'Gee, noised abroad for a Hercules in strength and an Apollo Belvidere for beauty, of a sudden is discovered all in a wretched heap; forlornly adroop as upon crutches, his legs looking as if broken at the cart-wheel. Solitude is the house of candor, according to Captain Kean. In the stall, not the street, he says, resides the real nag.

The innate disdain of regularly bred seamen toward 'Gees receives an added edge from this. The 'Gees undersell them working for biscuit where the sailors demand dollars. Hence anything said by sailors to the prejudice of 'Gees should be received with caution. Especially that jeer of theirs, that monkey-jacket was originally so called from the circumstance that that rude sort of shaggy garment was first known in Fogo. They often call a monkey-jacket a 'Gee-jacket. However this may be, there is no call to which the 'Gee will with more alacrity respond than the word "Man!"

Is there any hard work to be done, and the 'Gees stand round in sulks? "Here, my men!" cries the mate. How they jump. But ten to one when the work is done, it is plain 'Gee again. "Here, 'Gee you 'Ge-e-e-e!" In fact, it is not unsurmised, that only when extraordinary stimulus is needed, only when an extra strain is to be got out of them, are these hapless 'Gees ennobled with the human name.

As yet, the intellect of the 'Gee has been little cultivated. No well-attested educational experiment has been tried upon him. It is said, however, that in the last century a young 'Gee was by a visionary Portuguese naval officer sent to Salamanca University. Also, among the Quakers of Nantucket, there has been talk of sending five comely 'Gees, aged sixteen, to Dartmouth College; that venerable institution, as is well known, having been originally founded partly with the object of finishing off wild Indians in the classics and higher mathematics. Two qualities of the 'Gee which, with his docility, may be justly regarded as furnishing a hopeful basis for his intellectual training, is his excellent memory, and still more excellent credulity.

The above account may, perhaps, among the ethnologists, raise some curiosity to see a 'Gee. But to see a 'Gee there is no need to go all the way to Fogo, no more than to see a Chinaman to go all the way to China. 'Gees are occasionally to be encountered in our seaports, but more particularly in

Nantucket and New Bedford. But these 'Gees are not the 'Gees of Fogo. That is, they are no longer green 'Gees. They are sophisticated 'Gees, and hence liable to be taken for naturalized citizens badly sunburnt. Many a Chinaman, in a new coat and pantaloons, his long queue coiled out of sight in one of Genin's hats, has promenaded Broadway, and been taken merely for an eccentric Georgia planter. The same with 'Gees; a stranger need have a sharp eye to know a 'Gee, even if he see him.

Thus much for a general sketchy view of the 'Gee. For further and fuller information apply to any sharp-witted American whaling captain but more especially to the before-mentioned old Captain Hosea Kean, of Nantucket, whose address at present is "Pacific Ocean."